W9-BDK-941

Geordi and T'Lara jumped over the last row of boulders and almost fell into a meeting of the Red team.

Sidra Swan jumped to her feet. "Hey!" she yelled. "Stevens and Mirayo—after them!"

Now Geordi and T'Lara were running for their lives, bounding like kangaroos over the rocks and bushes. He turned to see that the two Redshirts were closing fast behind them, running with powerful strides. T'Lara was far ahead. She was headed toward one of those weird archways. His communicator beeped. He tapped it but was too out of breath to say anything.

"T'Lara here. Lead them under the archway. I will attend to them."

"Can't . . ." he gasped, "sacrifice . . . yourself!"

"I can," she answered. "If you lead them under the archway, I will know that is your wish."

Geordi's heart was pounding furiously and his legs were starting to give out. He had a choice—run under the arch and save himself, or let himself be captured and save T'Lara.

His comm badge beeped again. "La Forge here," he answered.

"Captain, it's Zemusta. They are attacking en masse! I count five of them, coming fast! I am falling back to our position. Out."

Wow! thought Geordi. After being taken by surprise, Swan apparently didn't want to take any more chances. She was going for an all-out blitz!

Star Trek: The Next Generation
STARFLEET ACADEMY

#1 Worf's First Adventure
#2 Line of Fire
#3 Survival
#4 Capture the Flag

Star Trek: Deep Space Nine

#1 The Star Ghost
#2 Stowaways

Available from MINSTREL Books

For orders other than by individual consumers, Minstrel Books grants a discount on the purchase of **10 or more** copies of single titles for special markets or premium use. For further details, please write to the Vice-President of Special Markets, Pocket Books, 1230 Avenue of the Americas, New York, NY 10020.

For information on how individual consumers can place orders, please write to Mail Order Department, Paramount Publishing, 200 Old Tappan Road, Old Tappan, NJ 07675.

STAR TREK
THE NEXT GENERATION®

STARFLEET ACADEMY™ #4

CAPTURE THE FLAG

John Vornholt

**Interior illustrations by
Todd Cameron Hamilton**

A
MINSTREL®
BOOK

PUBLISHED BY POCKET BOOKS

New York   London   Toronto   Sydney   Tokyo   Singapore

The sale of this book without its cover is unauthorized. If you purchased this book without a cover, you should be aware that it was reported to the publisher as "unsold and destroyed." Neither the author nor the publisher has received payment for the sale of this "stripped book."

This book is a work of fiction. Names, characters, places, and incidents are products of the author's imagination or are used fictitiously. Any resemblance to actual events or locales or persons, living or dead, is entirely coincidental.

A MINSTREL PAPERBACK *ORIGINAL*

A Minstrel Book published by
POCKET BOOKS, a division of Simon & Schuster Inc.
1230 Avenue of the Americas, New York, NY 10020

Copyright © 1994 by Paramount Pictures. All Rights Reserved.

STAR TREK is a Registered Trademark of Paramount Pictures Corporation registered in the U.S. Patent and Trademark Office.

This book is published by Pocket Books, a division of Simon & Schuster Inc., under exclusive license from Paramount Pictures.

All rights reserved, including the right to reproduce this book or portions thereof in any form whatsoever. For information address Pocket Books, 1230 Avenue of the Americas, New York, NY 10020

ISBN: 0-671-87998-7

First Minstrel Books printing June 1994

10 9 8 7 6 5 4 3 2 1

A MINSTREL BOOK and colophon are registered trademarks of Simon & Schuster Inc.

Cover art by Catherine Huerta

Printed in the U.S.A.

For Sarah and Eric

STARFLEET TIMELINE

2264

The launch of Captain James T. Kirk's five-year mission, <u>U.S.S. Enterprise,</u> NCC-1701.

2292

Alliance between the Klingon Empire and the Romulan Star Empire collapses.

2293

Colonel Worf, grandfather of Worf Rozhenko, defends Captain Kirk and Doctor McCoy at their trial for the murder of Klingon chancellor Gorkon.

Khitomer Peace Conference, Klingon Empire/Federation (<u>Star Trek VI</u>).

2323

Jean-Luc Picard enters Starfleet Academy's standard four-year program.

2328

The Cardassian Empire annexes the Bajoran homeworld.

2341

Data enters Starfleet Academy.

2342

Beverly Crusher (née Howard) enters Starfleet Academy Medical School, an eight-year program.

2346

Romulan massacre of Klingon outpost on Khitomer.

2351

In orbit around Bajor, the Cardassians construct a space station that they will later abandon.

2353

William T. Riker and Geordi La Forge enter Starfleet Academy.

2354

Deanna Troi enters Starfleet Academy.

2356

Tasha Yar enters Starfleet Academy.

2357

Worf Rozhenko enters Starfleet Academy.

2363

Captain Jean-Luc Picard assumes command of U.S.S. Enterprise, NCC-1701-D.

2367

Wesley Crusher enters Starfleet Academy.
An uneasy truce is signed between the Cardassians and the Federation.
Borg attack at Wolf 359; First Officer Lieutenant Commander Benjamin Sisko and his son, Jake, are among the survivors.
U.S.S. Enterprise-D defeats the Borg vessel in orbit around Earth.

2369

Commander Benjamin Sisko assumes command of Deep Space Nine in orbit over Bajor.

Source: Star Trek® Chronology / Michael Okuda and Denise Okuda

CAPTURE THE FLAG

CHAPTER

1

Starfleet Academy attracted only the best, the smartest, the most ambitious. They were young people who didn't fear outer space or the unknown. They didn't fear Romulans or Tholians. They wanted to command starships, space stations, planetary outposts, and have hundreds of people following their orders. Only failure at the Academy could stop them, and each cadet had his own secret fear about that.

Some feared subjects like trigonometry, exo-zoology, or quantum physics. Others worried that their superiors and fellow cadets wouldn't like them. Many feared that they wouldn't be able to pilot the training ships. A few were secretly homesick and didn't know whether they would be able to spend years away from home. Some feared that they just weren't good enough.

Cadet Geordi La Forge knew exactly what he feared the most:

Gym class.

Not that Geordi wasn't athletic. He was short but muscular, and he enjoyed physical activity. But there was something about the competitive nature of gym class that bothered him. He was confident of his own abilities, but he knew he looked strange with a Visual Instrument and Sensory Organ Replacement, or VISOR, covering his eyes. The high-tech device allowed Geordi to "see" the full electromagnetic spectrum, from infra-red to ultra-violet. In the classroom or the flight simulator, it didn't matter that he was blind. But in gym class it mattered.

It mattered right now because two captains were choosing sides for a game of elimination. Geordi wanted to be chosen first, but he never was. They took one look at his VISOR and wondered what good a blind man would be in a fast-moving game, and they chose somebody else. It had always been that way, until people got to know him.

But getting to know him wasn't easy. Geordi wasn't the outgoing type. He had only been at the Academy for three weeks, and he didn't even know the names of many of his fellow cadets. He was there to work hard and study—to learn to be a Starfleet officer. Everything else was secondary.

Still, it hurt when he was left at the end, after most of the thirty-two members of his gym class had been chosen. Glumly he looked at the unlucky ones who hadn't been chosen yet.

There was a chubby Tellarite, who snorted with his piglike snout whenever someone else was chosen. Beside him was a Vulcan female, who had to be the thinnest person Geordi had ever seen. Another female was human but albino, and she looked as delicate as a porcelain sculpture. A small Saurian with purplish skin and reptilian features stood next in line. The last of the unchosen was a dark-skinned Neo-pygmy from Africa. He stretched on his toes like a bantam rooster.

While the captains tried to make up their minds, the bunch of oddballs glanced at one another. Except for the Vulcan, their eyes betrayed the fact that they knew they were unwanted.

"T'Lara," said one of the captains.

Geordi sighed. The skinny Vulcan cadet had been chosen ahead of him.

"La Forge," said the other captain.

"Finally," Geordi muttered. He ran to join his teammates on the south side of the gymnasium.

A few seconds later everyone in the class had joined one of the teams. Geordi tried to tell himself that it didn't matter in which order they were chosen, but it did matter. *Everything at the Academy mattered.* It was only his first year, but he knew the instructors were taking notes and looking for leadership qualities. *How could you be a leader if you were always chosen last?*

He stood stiffly at attention in his white shirt and gym shorts while the instructor, Lieutenant Emma Pantano, explained the rules.

"I'm sure most of you have played elimination before," she began, "but I'll go over the rules. Each team must remain behind their white line. We have three soft inflatable balls, and the object is to throw a ball at the opposing team and hit one of the opposing players. You

3

can avoid being hit either by dodging the ball or catching it in the air. Once a thrown ball hits the floor or the wall, it's a loose ball and is safe to go after.

"Sensors will determine if you've been hit, and the computer will announce your name. If you are hit, you are eliminated and must go to the bleachers. When all the players on one team are eliminated, the other team has won. Are there any questions?"

How could there be any questions? thought Geordi. It was the simplest game he'd ever heard of. Yet it tested their survival instincts, physical skills, and teamwork abilities. He looked around the gymnasium and could see the hidden sensors through his VISOR. He knew they were recording video logs of the gym class. But he didn't know who would be watching those video logs.

That was the most nerve-racking part of Starfleet Academy—the idea that you were always being watched and evaluated. Being blind, he came in with one strike against him, but he knew he had to put that out of his mind. *Just do the best you can,* Geordi told himself. *They can't expect more from you than that.*

The computer sounded a loud tone, and the game began. Geordi had always been good at blending into the background, not standing out, making himself almost invisible. It was a trait he had to avoid in his classes at the Academy, but it served him well in this game. Plus, he had been one of the last chosen, and they didn't consider him much of a threat.

The other side had several strong players, and they hurled the inflatable balls with such force that there was no way to avoid them—unless you were almost invisible.

4

Three of his sixteen teammates were hit in the first volley.

"Mirayo, out," said the computer. "Takama, out. Swan, out."

Geordi didn't go after any of the balls that flew past him. His instincts were centered on survival. He let the captain of his team and the more aggressive players go after the loose balls. One of his teammates, a tall Andorian with blue skin and antennae sticking out of his white hair, grabbed a ball and threw it with a loud grunt. It hit a young man on the opposing team so hard that he sprawled onto his back.

"Stevens, out," announced the computer.

The action was furious. Geordi watched the Andorian move closer to the line so that he could catch the balls and throw them back quickly. *That isn't going to last long,* thought Geordi. Sure enough, the opposing team began to horde the balls until they had all three of them in their possession.

Their captain, a blond-haired human named Pettey, pointed to the Andorian and said something to his teammates. The three of them threw their balls at once. The Andorian caught one ball, one sailed over his head, but the other one struck him in the leg.

"Altos, out," intoned the computer.

His head hung low, the Andorian marched toward the bleachers. Geordi noted that the one who had hit him was the skinny Vulcan, T'Lara.

Half of the players on both sides had been eliminated, and Geordi hadn't touched a single ball. It was time to take an active part in the contest, especially if the opposition was going to target them individually. He grabbed

5

a loose ball just as a second ball zipped over his shoulder. It was the closest he had come to being hit.

On the other side Pettey was beginning to sense victory. He edged closer to the line to catch the balls as they flew across. Geordi had been watching the big human, and he knew that he was the key to the other side's victory. With his great reflexes, how could they hit him?

One of his teammates grabbed a ball, and Geordi pointed toward the Vulcan. They hurled their balls in unison, and Geordi's ball hit her on the ankle.

"T'Lara, out," said the computer. She showed no emotion as she strode toward the bleachers and took a seat.

But Pettey looked angry. He had a ball in one hand, and he pointed with his other hand at Geordi, as if he were going out next. He aimed low, and Geordi leapt over the ball to escape it. The ball banged off the wall behind him and bounced back to Pettey.

"Derlenger, out," said the computer. "Craycroft, out."

Geordi looked around and saw that he only had three teammates left—a stocky dark-haired young woman, a nimble Delosian, and the little Saurian. The other side had six players left. Worse, Pettey's team had control of the balls and were standing at the line and throwing them at will. They flung the balls with such force that they bounced back even if they didn't hit anyone. It was like shooting fish in a barrel.

Geordi was getting winded from bouncing around to avoid the balls. *If only we could get control of the balls,* he thought, *then* we *could stand at the line and shoot fish in a barrel.*

6

He turned to his three teammates and barked out an order, "Catch those balls!"

They nodded in agreement. They were all getting tired of jumping around like frightened jackrabbits. When the next volley came, they didn't jump but stood their ground. Geordi watched the ball zoom into his stomach—it knocked him off his feet, but he held on. The stocky young woman also caught a ball. The Delosian lunged for one but missed. He got hit, but the little Saurian reacted quickly and grabbed the loose ball.

"Gogarty, out," said the computer.

They were down to three, but each of the three had a ball in his hand. They walked calmly to the line, and Pettey and his teammates beat a hasty retreat to the far wall. Geordi knew exactly what he wanted to do next.

"Get Pettey," he whispered. The young woman and the Saurian nodded.

They hurled their balls in unison, and the big blond-haired kid didn't have a chance.

"Pettey, out," remarked the computer.

Pettey scowled at Geordi as he walked off the floor. He kept staring at the young cadet from the bleachers.

With their leader gone, the other team lost its confidence. Geordi and his teammates were able to stay at the line and pick them off one by one. It was the strong dark-haired woman who got the last one.

"All right!" she cheered. She clasped Geordi's hand and shook it, but he only smiled. The Saurian gave him a twisted grin.

Maybe next time they won't choose me last.

Emma Pantano strode to the center of the floor. The middle-aged gym instructor was also smiling. "That was

8

one of the best games of elimination I've ever seen. We're going to end a little early today because I have an announcement to make. Please take your showers, get dressed, and report back here in ten minutes."

"What's that all about?" Geordi heard someone say. There was a lot of talk as they headed for the locker rooms, but nobody seemed to know what the announcement was going to be about.

Geordi found himself walking beside Pettey. It didn't seem like an accident.

"You got lucky," Pettey grumbled.

"Maybe," answered Geordi. He looked up at the handsome cadet, who was a head taller than he.

"Next time," said Pettey, "I'll take you out first."

The big cadet shouldered past him and charged out the door. Geordi could only shake his head.

"Blowhard," said a female voice. Geordi turned to see the dark-haired cadet who had helped him win the game. "If you hadn't given that order, we would have been goners."

Geordi shrugged. "You played the whole game—I was only playing hard at the end."

"Still, it was a good thing you were there at the end. Good game!" She slapped him on the back so hard she nearly knocked his VISOR off. Then she headed toward the women's locker room.

The chubby Tellarite stood in the automatic doorway, keeping it open for Geordi. "Excellent game," he said. "We were proud of you."

Geordi knew who the "we" were—all the other cadets who got chosen last. That saddened him for a moment.

No matter how many games he won, he would never be like Cadet Pettey.

"Thanks," was all he could think to say.

After they showered and changed into their cadet uniforms, the gym class assembled back in the gymnasium. They sat patiently on the bleachers, waiting for Lieutenant Pantano to return. When she did, Captain Joe McKersie, the flight instructor, was with her.

"Next week's gym class is going to be rather unusual," said Pantano. "As some of you may know, Captain McKersie is leading a training mission for upperclassmen next week. What you didn't know is that you're going on that training mission."

There was excited murmuring in the bleachers, and Captain McKersie held up his hand to quiet them.

"You should know that you're going as passengers," he added. "Every year Lieutenant Pantano selects her best first-year gym class for this honor. While we conduct our training, you'll be let off on the planet of Saffair, where you'll conduct three days of wilderness and combat training."

Nobody could see the worry in Geordi's eyes, but he sat stiffly, waiting for more information.

Emma Pantano smiled slyly. "I think you'll find the game we play on Saffair very interesting. The planet has approximately one-half the gravity of Earth. Whatever you weigh here, you'll weigh half that on Saffair. You should be able to jump twice as far, run twice as fast. You're going to have a lot of fun, believe me."

She checked her watch. "I haven't got time to explain more now. Report to Transporter Room One at oh-seven-hundred hours on Tuesday morning. Your other instructors have been notified, and most of you will have to work all weekend to get a jump on your class assignments. If you have any social plans, you'd better cancel them."

Social plans, thought Geordi. That was something he didn't have to worry about. However, combat training sounded like something he should worry about, even if Lieutenant Pantano called it a game.

"Don't bring any luggage," she added. "Everything you need will be furnished. Class dismissed."

CHAPTER

The setting sun glinted off the water in San Francisco Bay and painted a golden sheen on the sleek buildings of Starfleet Academy. This was Geordi's favorite time to go walking in the gardens that snaked throughout the campus. It was late summer, but somehow the irises, crocuses, and daffodils were all still blooming.

Geordi didn't know what the colors of the flowers really looked like, but he could see their inner glow with his VISOR. It relaxed him. He was still excited from the gym class and the promise of his first training mission. But he was still worried about his future. Today he had won, but what did that mean? He would always be different from cadets like Pettey and the dark-haired young woman.

Geordi wandered off the path to get a closer look at

the stream that flowed through the garden. Its coolness actually looked blue in his infrared field of vision, and its soft babbling was like music. He was standing on the mossy bank when a voice barked at him:

"Get off my liverwort!"

Geordi jumped back and looked around for the source of the angry voice. A little old man in dirty pants rushed up and shook his spade at him. "That's not grass you're standing on—it's ground covering!"

"I—I'm sorry," stammered Geordi. "It all looks the same to me."

"Oh, I see," said the little man. "You must be La Forge."

"You know who I am?" asked Geordi in amazement. He hadn't met many people at the Academy who cared enough about first-year cadets to learn their names.

"Certainly," said the gardener. He bent down and tried to fix the plants that Geordi had crushed. "I know everybody here, and everybody knows me."

"You're Boothby," said Geordi, remembering the stories he had heard. "How come I never met you before?"

"You never stood on my plants before. That's a sure way to meet me."

Geordi smiled in spite of the man's grumpy attitude. "I'm really sorry."

"Well," said Boothby, "at least you have an excuse. The others are just plain clumsy." Content with his repair work, the little man stood up. "So how do you like the Academy?"

"Okay," answered Geordi.

"Only okay? Coming here is supposed to be the

13

chance of a lifetime. It's the greatest school in the Federation, so I'm told, and you say it's only okay?"

Geordi started to walk away. "I don't want to bother you."

"You don't bother me," said Boothby. "I'm nosy. That's how I know everything. You don't think you're gonna make it here, do you?"

Geordi shrugged. "Like you said, I have an excuse for making mistakes—I'm blind."

"So you have an excuse to fail," said Boothby. "To quit, if things get tough. I've got news for you, La Forge—the Academy is tough on everybody. I've seen them come and go. The high and the mighty. The ones you think can't miss *do* miss. The ones you think won't last a year go on to be admirals."

He looked down at his beloved plants. "Training Starfleet officers is a lot like gardening. You pick ones you think will do well, nurture them, and hope for the best. Sometimes they still refuse to grow. Sometimes the ugliest, scrawniest weeds do better than pedigree rosebushes. Am I making sense, La Forge?"

Geordi smiled. "Yeah."

"What's your major field?"

"Engineering," answered the cadet, touching his VISOR. "Technology has helped me a lot, and I want to give something back. I might also specialize in navigation."

Boothby nodded, and for the first time the old gardener smiled. "Selflessness—that's a good trait for a Starfleet officer. Remember, La Forge, this school isn't preparing you just for good times and high adventure, but for the bad times, too.

14

"There will be times when you'll get passed over for promotion, or you'll get an assignment you don't like. Or maybe you'll command a ship that's about to be torn apart, and all you can do is prepare your crew to die." Boothby pointed to the sky. "Remember, it's not just you out there."

Geordi nodded. "I'll remember. Say, do you know anything about the combat games they play on Saffair?"

Boothby chuckled. "You're going to Saffair, huh? Well, plant your flag high."

"Plant my flag high?" asked Geordi, puzzled.

"You'll know what I'm talking about. Now, I gotta get back to work."

Geordi started off. "Nice to meet you, Mr. Boothby."

"You, too," said the gardener. "But, La Forge, I don't care if you are blind—stay off my liverwort!"

In his quarters Geordi pored over his notes from a lecture on starship hulls in his Basic Engineering class. Tritanium, duranium, aluminum crystalfoam, ceramic polymers—so many materials and alloys were used in a starship hull, he didn't know if he could keep them all straight. Not only that, he had to learn how welding, bonding, forcefields, and warp speeds affected each one. *This will take a lifetime to learn,* he thought glumly. Maybe that was the point. Even four years in Starfleet Academy couldn't really prepare you to be a Starfleet engineer. Maybe it would only prepare you to keep learning for the rest of your life.

He took off his VISOR and rubbed his pale sightless eyes. *Oh, that feels good,* he thought. No one realized the concentration that was required to "see" with the complex instrument. He had to force his optic nerves to accept a variety of inputs that they were never intended to accept. Then he had to force his brain to interpret the strange impulses.

He stretched his arms and relaxed, looking around the room at total blackness. When Geordi allowed himself to be really blind, it was like taking a relaxing nap. By the luck of the draw, Geordi didn't have a roommate.

Maybe it wasn't luck, he thought suddenly. *Maybe they figured a blind man would be stumbling over a roommate.*

A knock sounded on his door. Geordi fumbled for his VISOR and quickly replaced it. He walked across the small but neat room and opened the door.

To his surprise, it was two of his teammates from the victorious gym team: the stocky dark-haired young woman and the tall Andorian.

The young woman barged right in. "La Forge, isn't it?" she asked.

"Yes," he answered. "Call me Geordi."

"Geordi." She smiled. "I'm Jenna Pico. This is Altos. He doesn't say much."

"Altos," Geordi repeated, and the big Andorian nodded in greeting. "What can I do for you?"

Jenna shrugged. "Well, a bunch of the kids in our class are getting together at the Bratskeller to talk about our upcoming mission. Want to come along?"

Geordi paused before answering. He had heard about the Bratskeller, a popular off-campus restaurant, and this was the first time anybody had asked him to go anywhere. Geordi wanted to go, but there was just one problem.

"I'd like to," he said, "but I've had an exam in Basic

Engineering moved up to Monday. I really have to study."

"Oh, come on," said Jenna. "All work and no play makes Geordi a dull cadet. Besides, you have to eat, don't you?"

"My treat," said Altos. He tried to smile, but his blue face only grimaced.

Well, thought Geordi, *it's not every day you get invited to dinner by an Andorian.*

"All right," he agreed. "But I can't make it a late night."

The Bratskeller was about six blocks off campus, and the cool evening air felt refreshing as they walked. It was good to see a cross-section of people, thought Geordi, not the usual bunch of somber cadets and busy instructors. Whether they were going out for the evening or were on their way home from work, San Franciscans always looked like they were having fun.

"This is great!" he enthused.

"Is it?" asked Jenna. "I grew up about fifty kilometers south of Frisco, so this is no big deal for me. Where are you from?"

Geordi sighed. "It would take the rest of the night to tell you all the places I've lived. I was born in Africa, but I left there when I was still in diapers. My parents were both in Starfleet—my dad was a researcher and my mom was a command officer. They tried to get assigned to the same stations, but it didn't always work out that way.

"I spent several years in the Modean system, where my dad was studying invertebrates. Then I spent time with my mom near the Romulan Neutral Zone."

"Not fun," observed the tall Andorian.

"Oh, no," said Geordi, "I thought it was great fun! I had the run of this giant outpost. We were trying to make the Romulans think there was this huge colony there, when there was really just a few of us and some jamming equipment. I was just a kid—I didn't know how dangerous it was. But the best times were when my mom and dad got assigned to the same ship. There were lots of ships."

Jenna sighed. "You sound like a natural for Starfleet. I'm used to this big city—I don't know if I could go to some lonely outpost for years at a time."

Geordi chuckled. "Funny, I was just as scared about coming here and leaving those lonely outposts."

"Home is where you hang your hat," said the big Andorian.

Jenna looked doubtfully at him. "I don't think you could wear a hat, Altos."

The Andorian touched one of his antennae. "No, but I could hang one right here."

The trio laughed as they continued their evening walk. They came upon an old tavern sign that was hanging over a stairway. The stairway descended under an old building.

"We're here!" announced Jenna. "The Bratskeller."

Geordi looked doubtfully at the stairs. "I know my vision isn't the same as yours, but this looks more like the entrance to a cave."

"*Skeller* means 'cellar,'" answered Jenna, starting down the stairs. "Just because it's underground doesn't mean the food isn't good. Do you like bratwurst and sauerkraut?"

19

Geordi gulped. "I don't know."

But he knew the German food smelled good as soon as Jenna opened the door. Altos ducked and went in after her, and Geordi followed them into the inviting darkness. He was still absorbing the strange sights and smells when they heard several voices.

"Jenna! Over here!"

Jenna was the popular one, and Geordi and Altos just followed along. Geordi was glad to see several of the cadets from his gym class, including the Vulcan, T'Lara, the Tellarite, the Saurian, and the albino woman. There was also somebody he wasn't glad to see—Cadet Pettey. He tried to ignore the tall blond cadet as he exchanged greetings with the others.

"Hello," he said to T'Lara.

The pointy-eared cadet nodded. "Hello, Cadet La Forge."

"Please call me Geordi," he said with a smile. "Uh, do Vulcans have first names?"

"None that you would be able to pronounce."

Geordi had never made small talk with a Vulcan before, but he was willing to try. "Are you excited about going on the training mission?" he asked.

"Excitement is not an emotion I allow myself," answered T'Lara, "but I am anticipating the trip to Saffair. May I ask you a question?"

"Please do," said Geordi.

"Without your VISOR, are you totally blind?"

Geordi had heard Vulcans were direct. "Yes, I am."

"It is not possible to correct your blindness by any means other than the VISOR?"

"Well," said Geordi, "some doctors have suggested

experimental procedures, but they all have a lot of risks. The VISOR works, in its own way, and it doesn't have any bad side effects."

"Very logical," agreed the Vulcan. "I believe you have a colloquial saying for such logic—'If it ain't broke, don't fix it.'"

Geordi laughed. "We have a lot of good sayings, but we don't follow them very often."

The tall blond man shouldered his way between them. "Hi," he said to T'Lara, "I'm Jack Pettey."

She nodded. "My name is T'Lara."

Geordi was completely blocked from the slim Vulcan's view, and he forced his way around Jack Pettey. "Hey," he said, "we were having a conversation here."

Pettey ignored him and grinned at T'Lara. "I didn't know that Vulcans went in for parties like this. What else do Vulcan females do for fun?"

"Fun?" she asked quizzically.

Geordi had a decision to make. Pettey had clearly cut in on their conversation, but there were plenty of other cadets he could talk to. Should he challenge the big kid or walk away? He looked up at the cadet's massive shoulders and knew he had to do something. But what? First, he had to get his attention.

Geordi took a deep breath and said, "I enjoyed beating you guys in gym class today."

That got his attention. Jack Pettey turned and looked down at the shorter cadet as if he were looking at a bug. "What did you say, pip-squeak?"

"La Forge," said Geordi. "Not pip-squeak."

Pettey squared his shoulders. "You know, pip-squeak,

we're not on campus here. Nobody can stop me from mopping the floor with you."

"I can," said Geordi. He could feel his heart thumping.

Conversation around them had stopped, and everyone was staring at them. If there was going to be a fight, Geordi was more worried about his VISOR getting damaged than anything else.

Pettey smiled, but it wasn't a pleasant smile. He used his height to tower over Geordi. "Let's go outside—just the two of us."

"I cannot allow that," said T'Lara calmly.

Jack Pettey looked down at her and sneered. "You stay out of this. He's been asking for it."

"A fight between two cadets from our class would reflect negatively on the entire class," she replied.

"Yeah?" he snarled. "And how do you propose to stop us?"

Then the Vulcan did something strange. She reached up to his neck as if she were going to pluck some lint off his collar. As soon as her fingers touched him, his eyes went wide. A second later the big cadet crumpled to the floor, unconscious.

"Wow!" gushed Geordi. "How did you do that?"

"Vulcan nerve pinch!" said the Tellarite, leaning over the fallen cadet. "Well done!"

T'Lara added, "The explanation requires considerable knowledge of the human nervous system."

"Never mind," said Geordi. "If I ever choose up sides for anything, I'm going to choose you first."

T'Lara cocked an eyebrow. "That would be logical."

CHAPTER

Tuesday morning was crisp, especially at 0700 hours. Geordi could see his breath as he walked across the commons toward Transporter Room One. It looked like bursts of blue in his infrared vision. He shivered a bit, because he had followed Lieutenant Pantano's instructions to the letter—he hadn't brought anything, not even a jacket. All he wore was his Academy uniform.

He could see other cadets converging on the transporter room from different directions. One of them was the Neo-pygmy, whose name he didn't even know. Geordi had never really seen how dark his own skin looked, but he couldn't imagine he was any darker than the small cadet who walked ahead of him. The Neo-pygmy was half as tall as Geordi, and Geordi considered himself short.

"Hey, wait up!" he called.

The small cadet looked around as if he didn't know he was being hailed. Then he finally saw Geordi jogging toward him.

"Hi," he said.

Geordi held out his hand. "Hi, I'm Geordi La Forge."

The cadet shook his hand eagerly. "Kareem Talo. Hey, you were really great in that game the other day."

Geordi shrugged. "I just stuck around long enough to do some good." He glanced at his watch—they were still several minutes early. "We can slow down and talk a while," he suggested, happy to make another friend.

"Okay," said Kareem. "I've been meaning to ask you—are you from Africa?"

"Originally, yes," answered Geordi. "But I left when I was very young. I've heard a lot of stories, but I'm afraid I don't remember anything about it."

Kareem sighed. "We Africans like to celebrate our diversity. Can you believe I was bred to be this short?"

"Well," said Geordi, "I know the Neo-pygmies take great pride in their heritage. After all, Pygmies are one of the oldest races on Earth."

"Yeah," muttered Kareem. "It was okay in Central Africa, where there are millions of us, but in this place I wouldn't mind being your height."

"I wouldn't mind having your eyes," said Geordi.

Kareem laughed. "Okay, so we're not perfect. So what are we doing here?"

"I'm doing what both my parents did," answered Geordi. "I really can't imagine what life would be like if I weren't in Starfleet. What are you doing here?"

25

"Trying to prove you don't have to be tall to make it in Starfleet."

"You don't have to prove anything," said Geordi. "Just be who you are, and do the best you can. That's what I keep telling myself."

They reached a door marked TRANSPORTER ROOM ONE and stopped. Other cadets hurried past them.

"You are wise, Geordi," said Kareem. "That's another reason I want to join Starfleet. I want to be wise. When I return to my town as an old man, I want the young people to look up at me and say, 'He has been places and seen things. He is wise.' "

Geordi grinned as they entered the room. "So let's go someplace and see some things!"

Their names were called in alphabetical order, and the cadets stepped upon the transporter platform in groups of six. When the operator saw they were all situated, he worked the controls, and they dematerialized in columns of shimmering light.

While Geordi waited for his name to be called, he noticed that some of the first-year cadets looked nervous, and he realized that the ones from Earth may not have transported before. He had been transporting all his life and couldn't imagine what they were feeling.

He glanced at his new friend, Kareem, who looked slightly paler than before. "Have you ever transported anywhere?"

"Once," Kareem whispered nervously. "When my family and I took a trip to Mars. That must've been ten years ago."

"There's nothing to it," Geordi assured him. "A little tingling, that's all."

"But don't people get stuck in those things? Or melted?"

"Only when the transporter is malfunctioning," Geordi answered. Then he smiled. "And that hardly ever happens."

Kareem gulped. "Hardly ever?"

Geordi's name was called, and he stepped briskly onto the transporter. *This is more like it,* he thought, *back to the life I know—the life aboard a ship.*

Within seconds he was standing in a smaller transporter room with gleaming silver walls instead of the dull plaster of a building. Geordi took a deep breath and felt right at home as he stepped off the platform. He spotted a lieutenant, who was checking the roster on a computer padd.

"Cadet Geordi La Forge," he said to the officer. "Permission to come aboard."

None of the other five cadets who had arrived with Geordi had said anything. The officer nodded, clearly impressed. "Permission granted, Cadet La Forge. I see that you've been on a starship before. Welcome aboard the *U.S.S. Glenn.* Please exit, turn to your right, and go to the lecture hall at the end of the corridor. We'll have a briefing as soon as everyone is aboard."

Geordi nodded and marched toward the door, which *whooshed* open at his approach. The others followed him.

In the lecture hall Geordi quickly spotted the big Andorian and took a seat beside him. "How are you doing, Altos?" he asked.

"Not so good." Altos bobbed his antennae and burped. "Still suffering from sauerkraut."

Geordi laughed. It felt good having friends, people he could share his experiences with. He looked around and saw a podium in the front of the room and several large overhead screens that were blank. In fact, the lecture hall looked just like a typical lecture hall at the Academy, only smaller.

He watched more cadets file in and look for seats. He waved to Jenna and Kareem when they entered, and he saw Jack Pettey as well. The big cadet looked none the worse for being unconscious a couple nights earlier. But Geordi noticed that he kept his distance from T'Lara.

Finally Captain McKersie and Lieutenant Pantano entered the room. The captain touched his comm badge, and Geordi heard him say, "McKersie to Bridge. Ship's complement is full. Take us out of orbit and set course for Saffair. Warp four."

Geordi looked around and estimated that there were about a hundred cadets. Thirty-two were from his gym class, and the others were mostly third-year students, none of whom he knew. A hush fell over the gathering as a slight hum indicated that they were moving out of orbit.

"Welcome aboard the *Glenn,*" said Captain McKersie. All conversation stopped completely. "This is a Meteor-class Starfleet cruiser that has been refitted for use as a training vessel.

"You are aware that we have two entirely different groups of cadets on board: my own Advanced Operations class and Lieutenant Pantano's first-year Physical Education class. The members of my class have their assignments, and they will be taking control of this vessel as soon as we are under way."

He put his hands behind his back and looked sternly around the room. "You first-year cadets are passengers. I want you to remember that. Your quarters are on Deck Three, and you are to remain on Deck Three. There's a recreational lounge on Deck Three, food slots in your quarters, and computer screens for reading. You are free to go anywhere you want—as long as it's Deck Three."

The older cadets laughed, and Geordi knew they were the butt of a joke. But he didn't mind. They *were* green cadets, and they didn't have any business trying to run things. He glanced over at Jack Pettey and saw the big cadet stiffening in his chair. *Patience, Jack. You'll get your turn.*

The captain continued: "On our return trip we'll give the first-year cadets a tour of the ship, but for now, you must let my class do their jobs. I will dismiss my class to take their stations, and the rest of you will stay to get your cabin assignments from Lieutenant Pantano."

He barked the order, "Class dismissed!"

At once two-thirds of the cadets filed out, talking cheerfully among themselves. Like most of his class-mates, Geordi felt envious, but he reminded himself that he would have a chance to be a starship crew member. He had to be patient now and remember that he was a first-year cadet.

Emma Pantano strode forward to address her class. "You heard what Captain McKersie said, and I hope you remember it. There is one thing you will enjoy on this trip—none of you will have a roommate."

There was relieved laughter, and Pantano waited until

it died down. "After I give you your cabin assignment, you are to go to one of the turbolifts outside this door. Just announce your destination, Deck Three, and you'll be on your way. For your information, this hall, the transporter room, and the Bridge are on Deck One. Crew quarters are on Deck Two.

"When you get to your room, you'll find a special uniform hanging in the closet. Try it on and make sure it fits. If it doesn't fit, hunt me down in the lounge to-night, and I'll get you a replacement. Report back here at oh-eight-hundred hours in the morning, wearing your new uniforms. We'll be beaming down to Saffair shortly thereafter."

Emma Pantano checked her computer padd. "Cadet Altos, Cabin three-oh-one. Cadet Baker, three-oh-two. Cadet Bushima, three-oh-three . . ."

Having the last name of La Forge got Geordi assigned to Cabin three-fourteen. The turbolift deposited him on Deck Three, and he stepped out to find himself in the recreation lounge. It was very impressive, with numerous game tables, padded chairs, music consoles, computer screens, exercise machines, and food slots.

No doubt, thought Geordi, he and his classmates would be spending a lot of time in the lounge during the next twenty-four hours. If they had to be passengers, at least they would be well treated.

He hurried down the corridor, anxiously looking for his cabin. When he approached the door of three-fourteen, it *whooshed* open. Geordi smiled, thinking of the clumsy doorknobs back on Earth. *This was more like it!*

Everything in the cabin was standard issue—single bed, food slot, sink and lavatory, a small dresser. It was

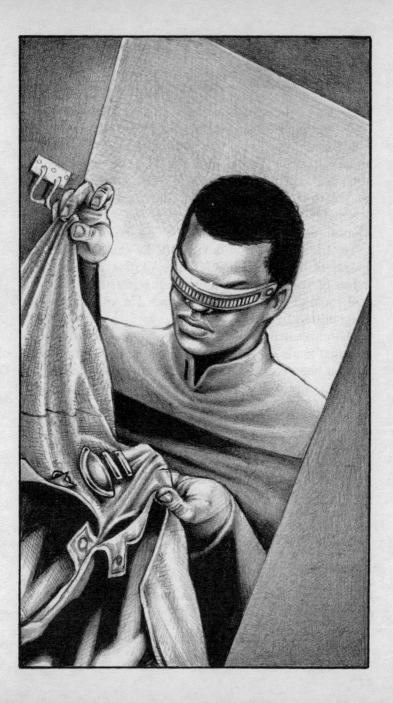

more compact than his room at the Academy, but that was all right. Geordi went immediately to the closet, curious about the special uniform that was hanging there.

At first glance there was nothing special about it. The color was brown, and the material seemed to be a bit thicker than his regular uniform. Then he pulled out the tunic and couldn't believe his VISOR. Stuck to the front of the shirt was an electronic device. It looked like a large emblem, about the size of his fist. *Strange,* thought Geordi. He had never seen anything like it.

He tried to pull the device off the shirt but saw that it was firmly attached. Geordi's VISOR let him get a sense of the inner workings of the instrument, but he still couldn't figure out what it was. He knew it was too complicated to be a decoration.

Also attached to the shirt was a communicator badge, and that made Geordi smile. It was the first comm badge he had been issued as a Starfleet cadet. He tried on the uniform, and it fit perfectly. Now if he could just figure out what that thing on his chest was supposed to do. . . .

Geordi changed back into his regular cadet uniform and went out to the lounge. He couldn't demand a tour of the ship, but he could study its specifications. From a food slot he got himself a glass of root beer, then he sat down at a computer screen to read engineering manuals.

Around him, cadets were listening to music, exercising, playing games, or just talking. None of them were wearing their new uniforms with the strange gizmo on the chest. He exchanged a few words with the other cadets, but he was more interested in finding out everything he could about the *Glenn.*

A few of the cadets who passed through the lounge seemed lost, as if they didn't know what to do with themselves. Geordi felt excited, but he also felt at home. He wondered why the others couldn't relax and enjoy the ride. Then he remembered what Jenna had said to him, that his upbringing made him a natural for Starfleet. Geordi had been so worried about his blindness that he never realized he was lucky in other respects.

Old Boothby was right. Nobody has it easy.

He turned off the computer screen and moved to a window to watch the stars blur past at warp speed. It was a familiar sight, but one that always delighted him. After a moment he felt rather than saw a presence sit down behind him. He turned and saw that it was the young albino woman—one of the misfits who had been chosen last during gym class.

"Hello," he said.

"Hello." She smiled. She really was like a porcelain doll, thought Geordi.

"I'm Geordi La Forge," he said.

"Megan Craycroft." She pointed to the window. "It's a beautiful sight, isn't it?"

"Yes," said Geordi. "I never get tired of seeing it."

"You've made a lot of trips at warp speed?" asked Megan.

Geordi shrugged. "I grew up in Starfleet. I think it's strange to look out a window and see trees."

Megan laughed, a hearty sound that didn't fit her delicate appearance. Then she grew serious. "I have to avoid direct sunlight because of my skin. So I think a career in Starfleet is a good choice for me."

"It's interesting," said Geordi, "how everybody seems

to have a different reason for wanting to join Starfleet. As a kid, you think everybody wants the same things you do. Now you see we're all different."

"Speaking of different," said Megan, "what do you think of that weird thing on our new uniforms?"

Geordi shook his head. "It must have something to do with the combat training on Saffair. I guess we'll find out soon enough."

Megan turned her head. "Look," she said, "there's Lieutenant Pantano. Should we ask her?"

Geordi turned to see the middle-aged instructor step off the turbolift. At once she was surrounded by curious cadets. He saw her smile and shake her head. Apparently, she wasn't going to tell them anything until tomorrow.

"My uniform fit," said Geordi. "How about yours?"

"Like a glove," answered Megan. "I think they know exactly what they're doing. The Academy doesn't make many mistakes."

Geordi watched the gym instructor walk through the lounge, saying hello to her students. The word got out quickly that she was present, and more students came out of their rooms and into the lounge. In a few minutes it was full.

But Emma Pantano didn't seem to want to make a speech. She just strolled around the room until she finally sat down by herself at a music console. She put on the headphones, leaned back, and listened to music.

Well, thought Geordi, *she might as well relax, too. None of us are going anywhere until tomorrow.*

Suddenly the ship rocked. People staggered to stay on

their feet. A piercing alarm sounded, and the room began to fill with smoke.

"Red Alert! Red Alert!" announced Captain McKersie over the intercom. "Battlestations! Battlestations!"

The klaxon alarms were deafening, and smoke was pouring out of the overhead vents. The cadets screamed and shouted, rushing in every direction. Geordi jumped to his feet and looked around the lounge for Lieutenant Pantano, but she was nowhere in sight.

"What can we do?" shouted Megan.

The ship rocked again. "Battlestations!" announced the captain. "We are under attack!"

"We've got to help them!" yelled one cadet, rushing for the turbolift. Whether they were trying to help or escape, several other cadets followed him. The turbolift doors banged shut behind them.

Instinctively Geordi looked out the window and saw that the stars were still. The ship had stopped moving.

CHAPTER

Geordi's heart was pounding, but he forced himself to remain calm. He remembered countless times as a kid when danger threatened his ship or outpost, and the only thing he could do was stay out of the way. This was just another one of those times, he told himself.

He got down on his knees to avoid the smoke, and after a few seconds he realized he wasn't even coughing. The smoke was thick, but it apparently wasn't deadly. Geordi crawled to the window to look out. He couldn't see more than a portion of the surrounding space, but he didn't see any attacking vessels. Who would attack them, anyway, this deep in Federation space?

"We've got to do something!" shouted Megan.

"No!" Geordi told her. "Just stay calm!"

Another cadet heard him and yelled, "But we're under attack!"

Geordi looked out the window again. There were no telltale flashes of phaser fire. If the *Glenn* was under attack, it wasn't returning fire. Geordi suddenly felt as if something was wrong, but it wasn't an attack.

"I don't know what's going on," he said, "but we're not under attack. Besides, what are our orders?"

"To stay on Deck Three," someone answered sheepishly.

"Right," said Geordi. He pointed to nervous cadets waiting for the turbolifts. "Get away from there!"

"Listen to him!" said a familiar voice. They turned to see Lieutenant Pantano striding through the smoke. She hit her comm badge and said, "Pantano to the Bridge. You may stop the simulation. How many disobeyed orders?"

"Nine," came the answer.

"Shoot!" muttered Pantano. She didn't look very happy. "That's worse than the last group."

Geordi noticed that the smoke had stopped pouring out of the vents, and the air was clearing. Also, there were no more alarms or jolts to the ship.

The turbolift doors opened, and nine very glum cadets stepped out. One of them was the Tellarite. They were followed by an ensign, who was entering their names on his padd.

Lieutenant Pantano glared at the nine offenders, who hung their heads in shame. "By leaving Deck Three, you disobeyed direct orders," she snapped. "You can be sure you will get a demerit for it. Three demerits, and you're out of Starfleet Academy!"

She turned to address all the cadets. "Things happen

suddenly on a starship. There's no time to think. There's only one way you can survive, and that is to obey orders. If you don't obey orders, you can see what happens—chaos!"

The instructor took a deep breath and seemed to calm herself. "I will admit, the captain did an excellent job rocking the impulse engines. I almost thought we had been hit myself. But there is no excuse for disobeying a direct order. None. Do I make myself clear?"

"Yes, sir," muttered thirty-two voices.

Pantano held out her hand, and the ensign handed her the computer padd. "This exercise had another purpose. Based on your actions under fire, I have selected my four captains for the combat games on Saffair."

She punched the names into the padd. "They are Cadet Geordi La Forge, Cadet Sidra Swan, Cadet Michael Takama, and Cadet Jack Pettey. Now, have any of you found that your special uniform does not fit?"

Nobody said anything, so Pantano nodded. "I'm sure you have many questions, and I'll address them all tomorrow at oh-eight-hundred hours. Don't be late, and be sure to wear your new uniforms. Get a good night's rest and—whatever you do—stay on Deck Three."

Pantano and the ensign strode into the turbolift and were gone. Geordi let out his breath. He didn't think he had done anything so wonderful. He had more experience aboard a starship, that's all. But he knew that panic never accomplished anything. Geordi was more worried about what it meant to be a captain in the upcoming games.

He looked around and saw Jack Pettey grinning at him from across the room. Pettey made a gun with his thumb and forefinger and pretended to shoot Geordi. Then he laughed and walked away. Nervously Geordi looked back out the window. The stars streaked past at warp speed.

The cadets were subdued the rest of the evening. Most of them took Lieutenant Pantano's advice and went to bed early to get plenty of rest. Geordi woke up refreshed and had breakfast in his cabin. Then he put on the strange uniform with the emblem on the chest. He was tempted to touch his comm badge to see if it was working, but he didn't want to risk getting into trouble.

Even in the corridor and the turbolift, there wasn't much talk. Everyone was thinking about the nine cadets who had panicked and gotten demerits. Everyone was wondering if there would be more demerits handed out before this training mission was over. It was one thing to sit in the classroom and study theory, thought Geordi; it was another thing to be tested under fire.

He entered the lecture hall and took a seat beside Megan, the albino cadet. She gave him a nervous smile. The cadets filed in quietly and took their seats. Several of them studied the devices on each other's chests.

Lieutenant Pantano entered the hall and took her place at the podium. All conversation came to a halt.

"Captain McKersie says we'll be going into orbit around Saffair in a few minutes," she began. "We'll be spending three days and two nights on the planet, living in tents. The *Glenn* will be in orbit around the planet most of that time.

"There is no intelligent life on Saffair and very little animal life. But there is a great deal of limestone in the crust of the planet. Chemical reactions with the limestone allow Saffair to have a breathable atmosphere, even though it only has half the gravity of Earth."

Pantano smiled. "But this isn't a scientific expedition. We're going to Saffair to play a game and learn something about combat, teamwork, and survival. The game you'll be playing is an ancient one called Capture the Flag.

"Our version involves no weapons, but it includes comm badges and a device called the coup meter. That's the thing on your chest. *Coup* is the French word for 'hit.' The idea comes from the Native American belief that it requires more bravery to touch an opponent in battle, and leave him alive, than to fight to the death.

"When an opponent touches your coup meter, you are automatically transported back to the ship. You are considered captured, and you're out of the game. The purpose of the game is to capture the other team's flag, which must be displayed in plain sight. It's that simple."

She continued: "Four teams will be chosen of eight cadets each. The playing field is two square kilometers. That sounds like a lot, but the game can cover great distances because of the low gravity. In the morning we'll beam each team up to the ship for final instructions and then down to an opposite corner of the playing field, where they will plant their flag."

Lieutenant Pantano touched her comm badge. "Teams can talk to each other over a secured channel on their comm badges. But your comm badges have limited range. If you try to hail a teammate and don't reach him, he's probably been captured and returned to the ship. Comm badges are the only technology you'll have.

"Today we'll just set up camp and get used to the gravity. Tomorrow there will be two elimination games. The next day the two winners from the first day will play for the championship. The two losing teams will play for third place."

Pantano smiled. "Now, if my four captains will come forward, we'll choose our teams."

Geordi felt embarrassed as he rose to his feet and walked down to the podium. Who was he to be captain of one of the teams? All he had done was show a little common sense when the fake attack started. Maybe, he hoped, there was a place in Starfleet for a cadet with common sense.

He took his place beside the other captains, trying not to look at Jack Pettey. *At least,* thought Geordi, *I won't have to worry about being chosen last.*

"When you are chosen, come down and stand behind your captain," said Pantano. "Mr. La Forge, you make the first choice."

That didn't require a lot of thinking. "T'Lara," he said, pointing to the slim Vulcan cadet. Pettey glared at him, and Geordi tried to ignore the big cadet.

The other captains, Pettey, Swan, and Takama, made their first choices. They were predictable choices—the biggest and strongest cadets in the class. Now Geordi had to make his second choice, and he was stumped. Did he want the biggest and strongest, the ones who were always chosen first?

Geordi smiled and pointed to the little Neo-pygmy. "Kareem."

Everyone, especially Kareem, was surprised. Jack Pettey snickered, but Kareem stuck his chest out and proudly joined his captain.

The others made their choices and looked expectantly at Geordi. He didn't let them down. "Megan Craycroft," he said, pointing to the delicate albino cadet.

Now everyone knew what Geordi was doing, and they weren't surprised when he pointed to the chubby Tellarite as his next choice. And they weren't surprised when he picked the small, purplish Saurian.

Geordi smiled at his team as they assembled behind him, and they smiled back. *Maybe we won't win,* he thought, *but at least we were hand-picked.*

When it came time for his last two choices, Geordi was relieved to see that Jenna and Altos were still available. He snapped them up. Even with the stocky dark-haired woman and the tall Andorian, his team was funny-looking compared to the others. But it was a happy team.

Emma Pantano looked from one team to the other, and a smile crept over her face when she saw Geordi's team. "Now, Mr. La Forge, you need to choose the color of your team," she said. "Your choices are Red, Blue, Green, and Gold."

"Green," answered Geordi. He didn't know what it looked like to others, but it was his favorite color.

Pantano nodded and took a small instrument from her pocket. She adjusted the instrument and touched it to the coup meter on Geordi's chest.

At once his shirt turned forest green.

All the cadets watched with amazement as she did the same thing to every member of the Green team. Their skins may have been many different colors, but their

43

tunics and coup meters were all the same. They were a team.

Cadet Swan chose Red for her team, and their shirts were transformed into a deep scarlet. Takama chose Blue, and their shirts became ocean blue. Pettey was left with Gold for his team, but he seemed happy with the color. With his blond hair and gold tunic, he looked like some kind of ancient warrior.

"You are now teams," said Lieutenant Pantano. "You will camp together, eat together, and plan your strategy together. I won't forbid you to talk to members of the other teams, but I suggest you don't. For the next three days they are the enemy."

She tapped her comm badge. "Pantano to McKersie. We're ready when you are."

"Fine," answered the captain. "We've been in orbit for about ten minutes, and the equipment and helpers are already down there. Send your first team to the transporter room. McKersie, out."

Pantano turned to her students and added, "One more thing. You can jump twice as high on Saffair, but you still have to come down to the ground. Don't go too crazy, or you'll end up with a broken leg or ankle. Green team, report to the transporter room."

Geordi nodded and glanced at his ragtag outfit. Kareem and the Saurian were about the size of little kids. The Tellarite was a blimp, and most of the others were beanpoles. But they were his chosen team.

"Come on," said Geordi, "let's show them."

CHAPTER

Geordi took his first step on Saffair without remembering the difference in gravity. He bounded a meter into the air, landed off balance, and promptly fell down. Jenna bounced behind him and lifted him up with ease.

"Come on, Captain"—she grinned—"you shouldn't look goofier than the rest of us."

But everyone looked goofy for the first few minutes as they bounced around like children in a playpen. The Tellarite, who had never been a lightweight before, was having the most fun. "Look at me!" he called, taking a leap and sailing through the air.

"Careful!" Geordi warned them. "Remember what the lieutenant said about coming down. I don't want to start out shorthanded."

"Yes, sir!" said Kareem, who promptly did a high flip

and landed on his feet. "See—no problem! Oh, I wish we could play basketball here—I could dunk one!"

Geordi laughed and shook his head. Well, he couldn't blame them for having fun. They were almost like a troupe of acrobats—leaping and flying all over the place. Altos, the tall Andorian, was the only one having trouble keeping his balance.

Hmmm, thought Geordi, by accident he might have done something very smart. *On Saffair, it might be better to have a team that's small and light, instead of big and clumsy.*

Geordi took some time to study their surroundings. This part of Saffair was a vast plain, with large, weird limestone formations. The limestone gave the soil and rocks a green, chalky appearance. There were no trees, just a few scraggly bushes. But, he decided, you could hide an army behind some of those big boulders and arches.

"Geordi!" called a voice. He looked over to see T'Lara standing on top of a large boulder, almost a hundred meters away. She jumped off the boulder and ran toward him with long, leaping strides. She covered the hundred meters in a matter of seconds.

"Wow!" said Geordi. "That's incredible."

"Not really," said the Vulcan. "Perfectly normal, given the relative gravity. Be careful when jumping onto the limestone—it crumbles easily." She pointed toward the boulder. "I believe I saw our camping equipment over there."

"Let's go," said Geordi.

Without planning it, the trip to the boulder became a

race. To Geordi's surprise, the albino cadet, Megan, beat all of them. T'Lara ran a close second.

"I have to get in the shade," explained Megan. "I can't stay out too long in this sun."

Atop the pile of equipment was an older cadet. He was fast asleep.

"Excuse me," said Geordi. "Are you our survival expert?"

He blinked awake. "Umm, are you guys here already?"

"It would appear we are," answered T'Lara.

The red-haired cadet staggered to his feet. "I'm Russ Wilmot. Pleased to meet you. Excuse me for sacking out, but I was up all night on the ops conn. Do any of you know anything about camping?"

"I do," said Kareem.

"Me, too," said Jenna.

Russ yawned. "That's great. Well, here are your tents. Put 'em up."

Under the guidance of Kareem and Jenna, the three tents were assembled. Each was supposed to sleep four people, but Geordi had his doubts. He assigned one tent to the three young women, T'Lara, Jenna, and Megan. He assigned another one to the two largest members of the Green team, Altos and Zemusta, the Tellarite. He took the third tent for himself, Kareem, and Vernok, the Saurian.

Russ Wilmot finally proved useful in explaining to them how to use the portable toilets and inflate the sleeping bags. He also explained how to prepare their food, which came in sealed pouches. By twisting the pouches, chemicals mixed and generated heat that cooked the enclosed food. The tuna casserole tasted surprisingly good, thought Geordi.

"Everything you see here," Russ explained, "is typical survival gear on a shuttlecraft. So if you ever crash-land a shuttlecraft, you'll get to do this all over again."

"Russ," said Jenna, "are there any tips you can give us about Capture the Flag?"

Russ smiled. "I'm not supposed to. I was on a team that finished third, so I'm not sure I could be much help, anyway. There are many different strategies. Remember, one or two people can cover a lot of ground. And to hit your coup meter, they have to catch you first."

No one interrupted him, but Russ wasn't going to say anything else. He looked toward a mountain range in the distance. Its strange spires and arches glinted in the setting sun.

"The sun goes down quickly on Saffair," Russ remarked. "You've got plenty of food and water. I'm sure you can figure out how to turn on the lanterns. We'll contact you when it's your turn to play. Well, good night. And good luck."

They thanked him, and Russ tapped his comm badge. "Wilmot to *Glenn*. One to beam up." A second later he disappeared in a sparkling column of light.

Now they were all alone on a strange planet, where the rocks were green and people jumped like kangaroos. Geordi looked across the barren plain and could see the lights of other encampments. Other teams. They could jog to one of those camps in a minute, but why? Lieutenant Pantano had been right when she had told them to stay away from the other teams. They were the enemy.

Geordi turned around and found every member of the Green team staring at him.

"Well, Captain La Forge," said Jenna, "what now?"

Geordi sighed. "Listen, you guys, if you aren't comfortable with me giving orders, we can choose somebody else."

There was a chorus of protest. "No way!" said Kareem. "We'll follow you anywhere."

"To victory!" bellowed the Tellarite, Zemusta. He crinkled his piglike snout.

Megan smiled. "That's right, Geordi. You made us all feel good about ourselves by choosing us first. Now you've got our loyalty, and you're stuck with it."

"Okay," said Geordi, "but we won't really rub it in their faces unless we beat them."

"So let's beat them!" crowed Vernok. It was the first thing the little Saurian had said all day.

Geordi nodded seriously. "All right. I've heard two pieces of advice that make sense. Somebody at the Academy told me to plant my flag high. Let's make sure we do that, because we don't want to make it easy for them to get it. Plus, if we put it on top of a formation with lots of arches and hiding places, we can lay in waiting for them."

He shook his head. "But those other teams have some strong people. If we get into a wrestling match with them, I don't know how we can score a coup first."

"Captain," said Zemusta, "I noticed that there are vines growing all over the rocks and ground. Perhaps they are strong enough that they can be woven into nets."

"Great idea!" said Jenna. "Even if it just slows them down for a second, it'll be worth it."

"Fine," agreed Geordi. "We'll divide our team into two parts—defenders and scouts. The defenders will get to work making nets as soon as we beam down. I think it's good advice that we only need one or two people to be scouts. Their job is to find the enemy's flag, and the enemy's troops, as soon as possible."

He touched his VISOR. "I may be able to see things with this that the rest of you can't. So I'll be a scout. Megan, with your speed you'd make a good scout, but you have to stay out of the sun. So T'Lara will be the other scout."

Geordi pointed into the quickening darkness. "Since T'Lara and I will be out there, I'm putting Jenna in charge of our defensive positions. Maybe Altos should be the last guy they have to get through. If I get captured, Jenna takes over. If Jenna gets captured . . . well, then we're in a lot of trouble."

There was laughter all around. When it died down, Geordi thought he heard a sound. All of the Green team members were gathered around him, so he didn't know what could be out in the darkness, scraping around.

"Did anybody hear anything?" he whispered.

"I did," whispered T'Lara.

Quickly Geordi grabbed one of the lanterns and shined it into the darkness. A furtive figure dashed away.

Kareem jumped to his feet. "A crummy spy!"

"Fiends!" shouted Zemusta.

"Let's get him!" snapped Jenna.

"I think he was just coming close when we started to

laugh," said Geordi. "But this tells us something—those other teams want to win as badly as we do."

"How can they spy on us?" asked Megan. "They haven't even told us which team we're playing."

"They're just trying to get an edge," said Geordi, "any way they can. They probably sent spies to every other camp. Nobody said we couldn't use spies."

"Or nets," whispered Jenna. She looked around. "I wonder where the actual playing field is. If we could get a look, it might help."

Geordi shook his head. "We're not going to go bouncing around looking for it in the dark."

"What are we going to do?" asked Zemusta.

Geordi shrugged. "Anybody know any good campfire songs?"

"Nah," said Kareem. "It's better to tell ghost stories around a campfire."

"No," said Altos, examining a pouch of spaghetti. "Better to eat."

In the end, everyone did whatever they felt like doing. While Kareem told African ghost stories, a few cadets ate, and others slept. There was no moon over Saffair, but the night sky glimmered with millions of stars. Geordi asked T'Lara to take a walk with him. He wanted to get to know the slim Vulcan who would be venturing into enemy territory with him.

"Have you any thoughts about what we'll be doing tomorrow?" he asked.

She cocked her head thoughtfully. "Only that we must be willing, and able, to outrun pursuers."

"Yes," said Geordi. "I had thought about that. That's why I picked you to come with me."

T'Lara nodded. "There are other reasons why I am a logical choice."

"There are?" asked Geordi.

"Yes. We Vulcans are stronger than we look. Strength may be very important tomorrow. Plus, you are our leader. You must be protected at all cost. If you give me an order to sacrifice myself to protect you, I will do it without question."

Geordi laughed nervously. "I don't think that will be necessary."

"It may well be," answered T'Lara. "Do not hesitate to ask it. As a Vulcan, I will sacrifice myself without feeling resentment. I am incapable of self-pity. When we locate their flag, it is imperative that you inform the others. You must be available to lead the attack." T'Lara looked straight ahead. "The needs of the many outweigh the needs of the one."

"All right," agreed Geordi with a shrug. "You can be my bodyguard."

"A good decision," said T'Lara.

Geordi chuckled. "I wonder if we'll play Jack Pettey's team? Wouldn't you like to beat him?"

She shrugged. "Beating the Gold team would be the same as beating the Red or Blue teams."

"Really?" asked Geordi. "You wouldn't like to beat him just a little bit more? He is a jerk."

T'Lara allowed herself the shadow of a smile. "As you say, he is a jerk."

That was all Geordi wanted to know. Deep down, he was both afraid and anxious to face the Gold team. He had never really hated anyone in his life before. Geordi wanted people to like him, and it bothered him that

53

someone didn't. But now he and Pettey were rivals, and there was nothing he could do about it—but beat him.

Later that night Geordi curled up in his sleeping bag. Kareem snored softly beside him. Vernok, the little Saurian, remained motionless on the other side, with no covers around his thick, reptilian skin. Geordi knew he had to sleep, but he couldn't. The excitement was too much. He had never pictured himself as a leader, but there was no doubt that's what his team thought he was.

I don't want to let them down.

He considered the eight members of the Green team: himself, T'Lara, Jenna, Megan, Altos, Kareem, Zemusta, and Vernok. They were all loyal and determined to do their best. What more could he ask?

With that comforting thought in mind, Geordi took off his VISOR and relaxed in the utter blackness. He was soon asleep.

Geordi was awakened by a strange beeping, and it took a moment to realize it was his comm badge. He sat up and tapped the badge.

"La Forge here!" He reached for his VISOR.

"Pantano here," said a familiar voice. "We've made a random selection. Your team will play the Red team in the morning match. You have an hour to eat and get ready, then we'll beam you up to the ship. From here, we'll beam you back down to the playing field."

"I understand, sir!" Geordi replied.

"Good luck. Pantano out."

Geordi rousted his teammates. "Get a good breakfast!" he told them. "We go in an hour!"

"I don't know if there's any food left," muttered Kareem. "I think Altos and Zemusta ate it all."

But there were plenty of packets of scrambled eggs, and even coffee. Nobody said much as they ate. The full impact of what was about to happen had just dawned on them. They were to be pitted against fellow cadets in a combat zone. The fact that there were no weapons didn't make it any less serious. What would the Academy think of the losers? What rewards would there be for the winners?

At least the day was fine, thought Geordi. Sunny but a little cool, with no sign of clouds. Considering the sparse vegetation, he didn't think it ever rained much on Saffair. After breakfast they practiced jumping, running, and landing—until the call came.

"We're beaming you up," said Lieutenant Pantano.

"Yes, sir," answered Geordi. He stood stiffly with his teammates until they had all dematerialized.

When they reached the transporter room aboard the *Glenn,* Geordi was surprised to see that Cadet Swan and her Red team were already there. Sidra Swan was a cocky young woman who stood several inches taller than Geordi. He could tell from the smirk on her face that she didn't think the Green team was going to be much of a problem.

Geordi glanced around at his team. Except for T'Lara, they looked more scared than overconfident. T'Lara merely looked alert.

Lieutenant Pantano produced two identical flags that were weighted at the bottom. One was red, and the other green. She handed them to the perspective captains.

"The flags must be placed in plain sight," she told

them, "within three minutes of your arrival. They cannot be moved after that. The boundaries of the playing field are clearly marked by white stakes. If you go outside the boundaries, or move your flag, your team will forfeit.

"During the game, many of you will have a coup scored against you. Because there's a slight delay in beaming up, simultaneous coups are not uncommon. If you get captured, you'll end up right back here. Just walk down the corridor to the lecture hall, and you can watch the rest of the game on the viewscreens."

She smiled. "We'll have some cold lemonade waiting for you. There will also be a medic to patch up your bruises. But remember, this is not a war—this is just a game. Don't get overly rough. A gentle tap on the coup meter is enough to dispatch the enemy."

Pantano consulted her padd. "By random draw, the Red team will be beamed down first. But they'll only have a few seconds' advantage. Before you go, I want both teams to shake hands."

Halfheartedly, the two teams shook hands. None of the players smiled.

"Red team, take the transporter."

Geordi felt his palms getting sweaty as he watched Cadet Swan and the Red team vanish from the transporter platform. His heart was pounding as he stepped upon the device. Jenna gave him an encouraging smile, but he could see that her fists were clenched.

"Coordinates locked in," said the transporter operator.

Lieutenant Pantano nodded. "Energize."

CHAPTER

6

Geordi landed in a nervous crouch. Immediately he began to look around for a high rock formation on which to plant the flag. This part of Saffair looked similar to the area where they had camped—except for the white boundary markers that stretched into the distance behind them.

"Start gathering vines!" Jenna ordered the others.

Kareem grabbed a long vine and wrestled several meters of it from the greenish soil. But he couldn't break off the last few centimeters.

"We don't have any knives," he complained. "How can we cut the vines?"

"No problem," answered Vernok. The little Saurian bent down and snapped the vine in two with his beak-like mouth.

Altos used brute strength to rip the vines from the ground. Zemusta, Megan, and Jenna collected the vines, stripped off the leaves, and began to tie them together.

"Use the thicker vines as a framework," said Jenna, "and use the lighter vines as the netting."

T'Lara tapped Geordi on the shoulder and pointed into the distance. "Captain," she said, "I believe that would be an acceptable defensive position."

Geordi followed her gaze to a weathered archway in the distance. The green rock looked like a giant doughnut that had been left outside too long.

"That's far away," said Geordi. "We only have a minute or so left. Can you reach it?"

"Yes," said T'Lara. She grabbed the flag from him and bounded off like a graceful gazelle. In less than a minute she had reached the top of the rock and planted the flag.

The others cheered, and Geordi felt like his heart would bounce out of his chest. "Okay," he said, "we'd better get some people over there to defend it."

"Altos, take the highest position," said Jenna. "Megan, you need to get out of the sun, so look for a cranny to hide in. The rest of us will gather a few more vines and come right over."

The Andorian and the albino dashed for the doughnut-shaped rock. Geordi's comm badge beeped.

"La Forge," he answered.

"T'Lara here," came the answer. "We are close enough to each other to maintain visual contact, as well as communications. I suggest we proceed into enemy territory."

Geordi took a deep breath. "Right." He may have

been the one in charge, but it was nice having people giving him good advice.

Jenna smiled. "We know what to do, Captain. We'll fight to the last cadet. You just find their flag and tell us what you want us to do."

"Is that all?" asked Geordi. He was trying hard not to be overwhelmed. He took one last look at his ragtag army and felt a burst of pride. They weren't pretty or impressive, but they wanted to win.

"If you're captured, there's no shame," he told them. "Just do the best you can."

"Yes, sir!" came the eager response.

Geordi looked toward their flag and saw Altos and Megan taking their positions on the archway. He tapped his comm badge. "T'Lara, let's move out."

"Yes, sir," she answered.

He saw the Vulcan woman leap off the archway and start running. Geordi began running as well, covering several meters with each stride. It felt good to be moving, but he reminded himself that the enemy was only two kilometers away. On Earth a person in good condition could run two kilometers in about ten minutes. On Saffair anyone could cover that distance in half the time.

He stopped and touched his comm badge. "T'Lara, slow down. We want to spot them before they spot us."

"Yes, sir," she answered. "Do you see the outcropping in the distance? It looks like a tower that is leaning."

"Yes," said Geordi. "Let's meet there."

A few seconds later Geordi and T'Lara crouched behind the oddly shaped rock. Geordi estimated that they had reached the middle of the playing field. He could just barely see some boundary markers in the distance. Thus far, there was no sign of any Red shirts.

There was no sound and no breeze. It was eerie—as if he and the Vulcan were alone on the entire planet.

"This is a quandary," said T'Lara. "How do we find their flag without being seen?"

Geordi smiled. "We have a secret weapon. I'm guessing that most of them will be gathered around their flag, just as we have done. I'm going to adjust my VISOR to look for a large amount of body heat."

"How do you adjust it?" she asked.

"Usually, in my head," answered Geordi. "There are a million impulses coming in—I just have to decide which ones to look for."

Geordi concentrated as he scanned the barren horizon. He was looking for a telltale haze of extra heat that might indicate several warm-blooded creatures standing together. Finally he found it.

He pointed excitedly. "Look! Oh, I'm sorry you can't see it, but there's a definite haze beyond that field of boulders. I think they've put their flag back there."

"That is not in plain sight," said T'Lara.

"Well, it might be if you were standing on the other side of the boulders. Anyway, something is giving off heat over there."

"We must get closer to confirm it," said the Vulcan.

"Yeah," Geordi muttered. "They know I've got the VISOR, and that might just be a decoy. This is a hard game."

"Ease of play is not the intention," said T'Lara.

Geordi sighed. "All right, let's go. If they spot us, we

61

escape together. Away from our flag. Let's not lead them to it."

The Vulcan nodded. "Understood."

The field of boulders was like a giant rock garden. Greenish lumps stuck out of the ground at irregular intervals. As he and T'Lara got closer, Geordi was dismayed to see that the boulders were rather large, some two meters high. That was more than big enough for a person to hide behind. The Red team had not planted their flag high, but they had chosen a good spot to defend.

He motioned to T'Lara to stop. "I have to check in with the others." He tapped his comm badge. "La Forge to Pico. Come in, Jenna."

"I'm here. Have you found it yet?"

"We think so," said Geordi. "There's a field of small boulders in the northeast corner. I think it's back there. But we have to go in for a closer look."

"Take your time," said Jenna. "There's been no sign of the Redshirts. Zemusta is our forward guard, and he has great eyes. Plus, we have our surprise all ready."

"Good," answered Geordi. "I hope it works. Out."

There were no great leaps and bounds now. Geordi and T'Lara crept forward through the field of boulders. Finally they saw their first glimpse of a Redshirt, jumping to the top of a boulder in the distance. Geordi and T'Lara dropped to their bellies and didn't move.

It was then that Geordi realized he had made another good decision by accident. Their green tunics blended in with the ground better than any of the other colors.

They lay there for several seconds, waiting to see if they had been spotted.

"Permission to offer advice," whispered T'Lara.

"Please," said Geordi gratefully.

"I can move swiftly. Let me run up there and see if their flag is present."

"You'll be spotted," whispered Geordi.

"I know. But it does not seem likely that we can sneak up on them without being spotted. Especially if their flag is in plain sight—behind a boulder. They are obviously playing a defensive strategy."

Yeah, thought Geordi, *they don't want to lose to the oddball team.*

"We'll both go," he said. "Two sets of eyes are better."

T'Lara nodded. They rose to their feet and began running at full speed. There was no pretense of hiding—they wanted to see what there was to see and get out. Geordi marveled at the way they covered a considerable distance in only a few seconds. They jumped over the last row of boulders and almost fell into a meeting of the Red team.

Sidra Swan jumped to her feet with a shocked expression on her face. "Hey!" she yelled.

Several members of the Red team scrambled to surround their flag, which was planted on the ground. One cadet made as if to move the flag, then stopped, obviously remembering the rules. The rest of them just stared at T'Lara and Geordi.

"Hi!" Geordi waved.

Swan shouted, "Stevens and Mirayo—after them!"

Now Geordi and T'Lara were running for their lives, bounding like kangaroos over the rocks and bushes. Within a matter of seconds T'Lara was several meters ahead of Geordi. He turned to see that the two Redshirts were fast behind them, running with powerful strides.

What a jerk you are! Geordi cursed himself. *You're going to be the first one caught!*

A minute later they were spread out across the ragged plain. T'Lara was far ahead, Geordi was about fifty meters behind her, and the Redshirts were gaining on him. He could see that T'Lara was headed toward one of the weird archways. Maybe, thought Geordi, she planned to make a stand there. Sure enough, she jumped halfway up the arch and scrambled out of sight.

Why are you stopping? thought Geordi. *Keep going—you can outrun them!*

His communicator beeped. He tapped it, but he was too out-of-breath to say anything. He just gasped.

"T'Lara here," came a voice. "Lead them under the archway. I will attend to them."

"Can't . . ." he gasped, "sacrifice . . . yourself!"

"I can," she answered. "If you lead them under the archway, I will know that is your wish. T'Lara out."

Even at half his normal weight, Geordi's heart was pounding furiously and his legs were starting to give out. He had a choice—run under the arch and save himself. Or let himself be captured and save T'Lara.

What had she said? *The needs of the many outweigh the needs of the one.*

He headed for the archway, still cursing himself for his stupidity. But he was their leader. Rightly or wrongly, his team was depending on him. He even slowed down to make sure his pursuers would follow him under the arch.

Geordi couldn't see T'Lara as he ran under the rock formation—she was well hidden. He wanted to stop and

64

help her fight, but he knew her ambush depended on surprise. He was about forty meters ahead of the Red players, so he stopped when he got that far beyond the archway. He fell to his knees, gasping for air.

He saw T'Lara leap off the arch and take one Redshirt by complete surprise. He vanished like a ghost. The other one attacked her, and they began to wrestle. In an instant they were both gone.

A simultaneous coup.

Geordi collapsed onto his back and just breathed for several moments. Nobody was after him now, and he knew where their flag was. He supposed their mission had been a success.

But he missed T'Lara.

His comm badge beeped. "La Forge here," he answered.

"Captain, it's Zemusta. They are attacking en masse! I count five of them, coming fast! I am falling back to our position. Out."

Wow! thought Geordi. After being taken by surprise, Swan apparently didn't want to take any more chances. She was going for an all-out blitz! Because it was high up on an archway, the Green flag hadn't been hard to find.

Geordi was torn about what to do next. After that long chase, he figured he was much closer to the Green flag than the Red flag. Should he go back to help them defend? It was six defenders against five attackers— almost an even battle. Counting the two T'Lara had taken out, that left one Redshirt guarding their flag.

Geordi couldn't stand it—he had to see how his defenders were doing. If the Red attack was successful, he would never be able to get back to the Red flag in time.

He skirted along the boundary markers until he could see the giant doughnut in the distance.

The battle was raging. Redshirts were climbing up the rock like ants. But he could see the small defenders jumping out of hiding places, throwing nets. Not all of the nets worked, but some of the attackers tumbled to the ground, thrashing about in the nets. They were easy prey for Jenna, Kareem, and the others.

Then Jenna was captured. Megan disappeared. Kareem was gone. Two Redshirts were left, and they fell back to regroup. He could see Altos, standing in front of their flag at the top of the archway. The last obstacle. He could hear Zemusta, who was laughing and taunting the Red team. He saw Vernok scrambling around.

Then Geordi saw something else. Another Redshirt was running across the plain to join his comrades for one last assault.

Their flag was unguarded!

Geordi hit his comm badge. "La Forge to Altos. You've got to hold them off! Their flag is unguarded. I'm going to get it!"

"Aye, Captain!" came the reply. "They get no flag over me."

Geordi ran across the plain faster than when he was being chased. Each stride gobbled up chunks of land. He could see the field of boulders in the distance. He could smell victory in every painful breath he took.

Then came a beep on his comm badge. "Altos to La Forge. Better hurry. Just me and one of them left!"

Geordi did hurry. He bounded over the rocks like demons were chasing him. Once he came down at an awkward angle and rolled onto his back, but he scram-

bled to his feet and kept going. When he finally spotted the unguarded Red flag, it was so beautiful it was like a mirage. He bounded over the boulders like a wild man.

He dived the last few meters and cradled the flag in his arms. He hit his comm badge, yelling, "I've got it!"

He was answered by labored breathing. Finally the deep voice of Altos replied, "No problem, Captain. Nobody left but you and me."

CHAPTER
7

Sidra Swan shook Geordi's hand, but she refused to smile. "Good game," she muttered.

"A close game," he replied. "You almost won."

She scowled. "We would've won, if it hadn't been for those damn nets. That crazy Saurian wrapped me up so tightly, I couldn't move."

"Sorry," said Geordi.

Sidra finally cracked a smile. "The nets were a great strategy, especially with your flag up high like that. It was so frustrating to see your flag but not be able to reach it. What did you think of the game?"

Geordi shook his head. "To me, the whole thing went by in a blur. I never got close enough to anyone to worry about a coup. I watched the decisive battle from a distance. All I did was run from one end of the field to the other."

"But you won," said Sidra. "That's the important thing." She glanced around the lecture hall. "They don't look it, but you picked a good team."

Geordi looked at his ragtag team, and his chest swelled with pride. Jenna, Megan, T'Lara, Altos, Kareem, Zemusta, and Vernok were eagerly reliving the game as they talked with members of the Red team. Like their captain, the Red team was glum, but they had a lot to be proud about, thought Geordi. Every single one of them had gone down fighting.

In fact, except for him and Altos, every single player in the game had been captured and beamed back to the *Glenn*. They had all fought hard. Harder than he.

Still, Geordi reminded himself, *I was the one at the end with the enemy flag in my hand*.

He took a sip of his lemonade. It was over now, and they could all relax. As a special treat, Lieutenant Pantano was going to allow them to watch the match between the Blue and Gold teams on the viewscreens. Geordi was looking forward to it, because he really did feel as if he had missed most of the action.

Three overhead screens blinked on, and the voices in the hall began to hush. The game had begun. One screen showed the Gold team scurrying to find a place to plant their flag. The other screen showed the Blue team, just beaming down. The middle screen scanned the empty middle of the playing field.

Emma Pantano entered the room and took a seat. "Relax," she told the cadets. "I suspect you'll enjoy this game more than the one you just played. In case you're wondering, I'm giving these teams a chance to review your game later on tonight."

She smiled. "By tomorrow everyone will know how to make nets."

Geordi took a seat in an empty row. Seconds later Jenna took the seat to his left, and T'Lara took the seat to his right. He smiled at Jenna, who grinned back. T'Lara was too busy watching the viewscreens to look at him. *They really are my lieutenants,* thought Geordi. *My left and right hands.*

"What are they doing?" whispered Jenna. She pointed to the Gold team.

With his mop of blond hair Jack Pettey was easy to spot as he leapt over some tall rocks and landed in front of a white corner boundary marker. He planted the Gold flag directly in front of the marker.

"Clever," said T'Lara. "There is only one way to approach the flag—head-on. If the attackers aren't careful, they risk going outside the boundaries and forfeiting the game. Plus, the Blue team has to cover the maximum amount of ground to reach the Gold flag."

Geordi turned his attention to the Blue team on the other screen. One of them must have talked to old Boothby, too, because they were planting their flag on a tall limestone formation. But it wasn't as high or as easy to defend as the archway T'Lara had picked.

Kareem leaned over Geordi's shoulder and whispered, "I'll give two-to-one odds on the Blue team. Any takers?"

Geordi shook his head. Nobody wanted to bet against the Gold team. They already looked confident and in command. Pettey had stationed his three biggest players near the flag to guard it. Considering there was only one angle from which the flag could be approached, that would probably be enough.

Led by Pettey himself, the rest of them fanned out and began a determined search for the Blue flag. Geordi noticed that the Blue team was wasting valuable time having a discussion. Just like the Red team had done. Considering that each team had the entire night before to plan its strategy, that was foolish.

Finally the captain of the Blue team, Mike Takama, sent three of his teammates to find the Gold flag. Of course, he didn't know they would be running into five enemy players. The Goldshirts were running at full speed, eating up several meters with each stride. Everyone's attention shifted to the middle viewscreen, where a major battle was taking shape.

In her excitement Jenna gripped Geordi's arm. He smiled at her. "Are you nervous?"

"Sorry," she said. "I was thinking of the Red team when they rushed us. I don't think I've ever been more scared."

"But we beat them," Geordi reminded her.

"Yeah," she said. "Nothing like surprise. We won't have that next time."

No, thought Geordi glumly. *Surprise is a weapon you can only use once.* The Red team had been overconfident, certain that brute force could beat a bunch of misfits. Tomorrow they would be playing for the championship, and no one would take the Green team lightly.

On the barren plain the two attacking forces were running so swiftly at half-gravity that they almost crashed into each other. The action was furious. The Blue team was outnumbered three to five, but they were closer together. Pettey's five attackers were spread out. The Blue attackers ganged up on a Gold player, hit his coup meter, and sent his molecules packing.

But the other Gold players swiftly converged on them. They heard Pettey scream like a banshee as he leapt over a rock and tackled a Blue player. He rolled the Blueshirt onto his back and slapped his chest. And the cadet was gone.

Another Blue player fought valiantly and scored a simultaneous coup, taking one of the Gold players with him. The other one ran for his life and was quickly brought down by two Goldshirts. He disappeared in a swirling mass.

Geordi turned his attention to the door of the lecture hall. Looking dazed and humbled, three Blue team members and two Gold team members walked in. Geordi didn't know yet what it felt like to be captured. Judging by the expressions on their faces, it didn't feel good.

"How about four-to-one odds?" asked Kareem.

There were no takers. Pettey still had three members of his attacking force left, counting himself. They moved cautiously forward, trying not to be spotted.

On the other screen the Blue team was in disarray. Takama kept trying to contact his three scouts, but it soon became obvious that they were no longer in the game. Unlike the observers in the lecture hall, he didn't know what had become of them until they were gone.

He turned to a strapping Delosian. "Take a wide route around," he told him. "Not through the middle. See if you can find their flag. If you find it, go for it."

"That is a mistake," T'Lara whispered to Geordi. "He must realize he is fighting a defensive battle at this point. To waste one of his best players is illogical."

Jenna disagreed. "Yeah, but he's got to find out what's going on. As we found out, it only takes one person to capture a flag."

"True," said T'Lara, "when there are no defenders."

"Maybe the Blue team can come back," said Geordi. "They only have one less player."

T'Lara nodded. "Also true. But the Blue team is strategically unbalanced. They have one attacker and four defenders. By contrast, the Gold team is balanced. They have three defenders and three attackers. They are prepared for any contingency."

Geordi sighed and slumped down in his chair. Half of him wanted to play the Gold team for the championship, and half of him didn't. He marveled at the way this game was completely different from the one they had played only an hour before.

Because the Blue flag was planted high, Pettey and his two teammates had no trouble finding it. Geordi thought that Takama had done a good job positioning the Blue defenders. They waited at different levels of the limestone formation. The husky Asian stood on top, guarding the flag himself.

"They can't go straight at it," said Jenna. "What is Pettey going to do?"

"A frontal assault would be risky," agreed T'Lara. "He could lose his advantage."

Kareem added, "His main advantage is that he knows how that last battle came out, and Takama doesn't. To know the enemy's strength—when they don't know yours—is a major advantage."

Pettey huddled with his teammates behind a rock and

discussed the situation. Geordi leaned forward to listen to the audio.

"Let's rush them," said one of the Goldshirts. "We can take them!"

"Not so fast," answered Pettey. "You never attack high ground unless you outnumber them. I count four of them, so they must have sent one man after our flag. I'm not worried about him. But if they sent one guy out, they might think we would do the same thing."

"Yeah?" asked one of his teammates. "What good does that do us?"

Pettey smiled. "You'll be willing to sacrifice yourself for the good of the cause, won't you? I want you to run up there and act like you're going to attack them all by yourself. Yell at them, throw rocks at them—I don't care what you do. But get them to chase you."

Geordi leaned forward. Here was Pettey ordering his teammate to do what T'Lara had willingly volunteered to do. It made Geordi realize how lucky he was to have the young Vulcan on his team.

Pettey was grinning. "If you can get two of them to chase you," he said, "it'll be even odds for Pete and me. Two against two. If either one of us scores a coup, we win. I'll take those odds."

Behind him, Geordi heard Kareem grumble, "Yeah, he's the only one who will take any odds."

T'Lara tapped Geordi's shoulder. "Over here," she said, pointing to the screen on the right.

The Gold defenders had spotted the lone Blueshirt who was trying to sneak up on them. Two of them set out in pursuit. Geordi watched the chase, remembering how he had been chased like that. It wasn't a pleasant experience. If it hadn't been for T'Lara, he would've been the first one to be captured.

After a minute or so the Goldshirts broke off the chase and returned to guarding their flag. They weren't too worried about an attack when it was three against one. The lone Blueshirt slumped to the ground, panting for breath.

Geordi turned his attention to the other screen, where the scene was replayed in reverse. Now a lone Gold player ran in front of the Blue defenders and taunted them.

"Hey!" he yelled. "You aren't so tough! We've gotten rid of all the people you sent out so far!"

"If you're so great," answered Takama, "come on up here!"

"Are you scared of me?" the Goldshirt yelled. "When it's four against one!"

Jenna grabbed Geordi's arm again. "They're not falling for it."

Then Takama made his fatal mistake. He leapt down from the limestone formation and started to chase the intruder himself. One of his teammates came to his aid, and there were only two Blueshirts guarding the flag.

Two Gold attackers appeared out of nowhere and began bounding up the rock toward the Blue flag. A Blue defender jumped on one of the attackers, and they hit the ground hard. Both of them disappeared in a cloud of swirling lights.

That left Jack Pettey one-on-one against a defender who was much smaller than he. Pettey grinned as he walked toward him.

The Blueshirt hit his comm badge. "Help! Help!" he yelled.

Takama came running back, but it was too late. Pettey bounded up the slope and hit the defender's coup so hard that the Blueshirt tumbled off the rock. Luckily he disappeared before he hit the ground.

Geordi slumped back in his seat, his heart pounding and his mouth hanging open. *That guy isn't human—he's an animal!*

Pettey swaggered up to the flag and clutched it like it was a trophy.

"Yeah!" he bellowed.

A buzzer sounded, and the screens went blank.

Lieutenant Pantano rose to her feet. "Hmmm," she said, "a rather one-sided victory. All in all, it's been an interesting day. Your supplies have been replenished, so you can return to your camps. The championship game between Green and Gold will be held tomorrow morning. The match for third place will be held in the afternoon. You are dismissed."

Geordi gulped and stood slowly. There hadn't been much time to savor their victory, he thought glumly. He looked at Jenna, who shook her head.

"We've got our work cut out for us," she said.

CHAPTER

With a stick Geordi drew a square in the chalky ground. His teammates were gathered around him, watching intently. The only one missing was Zemusta, who was standing guard in case the enemy decided to send spies to their camp. The sun was slipping quickly behind the mountains of Saffair.

"Here's the playing field," he said, pointing to the square. He drew two X's in opposing corners. "There are the flags. In our match the major battle took place around our flag. That's just too risky. If Altos hadn't scored that last coup, we'd be playing for third instead of first place tomorrow."

He plunged the stick into the middle of the square. "This is where the Gold team won their match—in the middle of the field. After that, they had all the advantages and none of the risks. It was just a matter of time. This is where we have to win tomorrow—in the middle."

"But, Captain," said Kareem, "they're so much bigger than we are. I don't think we can beat them on the open ground, even with nets."

There were murmurs of agreement. Geordi waved them off. "I wasn't thinking of a fair fight. I was thinking of an ambush."

He glanced at T'Lara. "It wasn't planned, but T'Lara and I staged an ambush in the middle of the field. It worked beautifully. The Red team lost two players to our one. If we can pull off a successful ambush, we'll get an advantage in numbers. After that, the Gold team will have to play more cautiously."

The Vulcan cocked her head. "There is a strong probability that the Gold team will use the same strategy that was successful for them today. They will keep a few people back on defense and rush us with the bulk of their force."

"Right!" said Jenna. "And they'll expect *us* to use the same strategy that won for us. They've seen the log of our game, so they know that we kept most of our people back, making nets. They won't be looking for us in the middle of the field."

"Now you're getting the idea!" said Geordi.

Megan frowned. "But we'll have to rush out there and find hiding places. We won't have time to make any nets."

Geordi scratched his chin. "Yeah, I had thought about that. I don't know how effective the nets will be if we try to use them again. That's why I was looking for some new kind of surprise. I'm open to suggestions."

Vernok opened his beak and started to speak, then the little Saurian grew quiet.

"Go ahead, Vernok," said Geordi. "We should all feel free to speak our minds. What were you going to say?"

"I am small," said Vernok. "Not so good in battle."

"But you wrapped up Sidra Swan like a birthday present!" said Jenna. "That was cool."

Vernok grimaced, or maybe it was a smile. "I was lucky," said the Saurian. "I have noticed that our flag and our uniforms are the same shade of green. If I turn my back to you and lower my head—do I not look like our flag? I can raise my elbow to let the wind blow my sleeve."

He demonstrated, and Geordi sat forward eagerly.

"From a distance, you *would* look like a flag," he agreed. "But how long can you hold that position?"

"We are a cold-blooded species," said the Saurian. "By nature we conserve our body movement. In other words, sitting perfectly still is something I do very well."

"Okay," said Geordi, "then we'll use you as a decoy. Altos, when we beam down tomorrow, you take our real flag and put it at the farthest corner boundary marker you can find. Just like the Gold team did with their flag. Then you hide and guard it. Vernok, you'll climb up one of the limestone formations and plant yourself at the top. Then pretend to be a flag."

He turned to Megan. "You go with him, and make sure you're very visible. Let them see you making a net. I don't know how you can look like more than one person, but you'll have to try."

"I'll tie my hair back," she offered. "I'll use leaves from the vines to make my hair look a different color."

"Great!" said Geordi. "That will leave five of us to stage our ambush. If they use the same strategy they used today, they should be coming with five attackers. We can't plan the ambush until we see the terrain. But we know what direction they'll be moving, once they see our decoy." The Green captain sighed. "It sounds complicated. I just hope all of its works."

Jenna added, "One thing that's very important is that we treat the decoy like our flag. If the ambush doesn't work, or you get separated, retreat to the decoy. Not the real flag."

"That'll be easy," said Kareem. "None of us will know where the real flag is, except for Altos."

The big Andorian twitched his antennae. "No one will get past me," he promised.

Geordi sat back in the green dirt and stretched his legs. "Okay," he said, "we have a plan. We'll find out tomorrow if it works."

He looked up in time to see the last slivers of sunlight disappear behind the craggy mountains. Gloom fell over the camp, and Jenna began to light the lanterns. Altos searched through the pouches of food, looking for his favorite dishes. No one had anything else to say.

Geordi was startled when his comm badge beeped. "La Forge here," he answered.

"This is Zemusta," came the reply. With amazement he said, "Jack Pettey is standing in front of me."

"Did you catch him spying?" asked Geordi.

"No. He walked up to me and said he wanted to meet with you. He's alone."

Geordi looked around at his teammates, but their expressions were as puzzled as his. "Send him to us," said Geordi.

"Yes, sir. Zemusta out."

Jenna frowned. "He probably wants to pick our brains. Nobody tell him anything."

Geordi looked at the diagram he had drawn in the dirt. He wiped it out with his hand. "Maybe he just wants to be friendly."

"Right," said Jenna doubtfully.

There was no mistaking the tall, blond-haired kid who strode out of the darkness. He could have bounded several meters at a time, but he seemed to be moving slowly on purpose. He acted like he didn't want to alarm them.

"Hi," said Jack Pettey with a big grin. "I just thought I'd join you for dinner. What have you got?"

Altos pulled a package out of the box. "Beef stew? I would guess you are a meat-eater."

"Good guess," said Pettey.

Altos tossed him the pouch, and he twisted it to heat the stew. Normally, Geordi hated to be unfriendly to anyone. But this was the enemy, in more ways than one.

"I watched the log of your match," said Pettey, seating himself out of T'Lara's reach. "Very impressive. I never would've thought of making nets. I'm sort of a brute-force guy."

Geordi smiled. "We noticed."

"Still," said Jenna, "you used trickery to win. You got Takama to chase that one guy you sent to taunt him."

Pettey shrugged. "If the enemy is stupid, you've got to exploit it. That won't be the case with you guys tomorrow. You didn't make any mistakes. Plus, you've got a built-in advantage."

"We do?" asked Kareem.

"Sure," said the blond kid. "La Forge's VISOR."

Geordi shook his head. "I never thought that being blind was an advantage."

"I watched the log," answered Pettey. "You and the Vulcan went right toward their flag. You didn't have to look for it. Are you gonna tell me that wasn't because of your VISOR?"

"It doesn't give me X-ray vision," said Geordi. He was going to explain that he only detected some excess heat, and it turned out to be the Red team having a meeting. But he stopped himself. *That's what Pettey wants—to find out what advantage the VISOR gives me.*

Pettey scowled. "You can't deny that you have a piece of electronic equipment that we don't have."

Geordi smiled. "Would you like to have a VISOR? I'm sure Lieutenant Pantano could make one from the replicator aboard the ship."

"Yeah!" said Pettey righteously.

"Before we do that," Geordi added, "why don't you try on my VISOR to see how you like it?"

There were a few gasps as Geordi took off his VISOR, and he remembered that his pale, sightless eyes looked strange to most people. He held the VISOR out for Pettey to take. Then he waited. It wasn't long before he heard a horrified scream.

"Yoww!" shouted Pettey, yanking off the VISOR. "Man, that thing is like knives sticking into your brain!"

"Yes," agreed Geordi. "It took me several years to get over the headaches. Several more years to sort out and interpret all the signals. If you started right now,

you might master it in a few years. Do you still want a VISOR?"

"No," answered the big cadet. "I, uh, I'm really sorry I bothered you."

Geordi put the VISOR back on, and he saw that the Gold captain really did look sorry. "Jack," he said, "I know we've had our differences, but we are different people. We'll never be very much alike. But we want the same thing—to be in Starfleet. In that way we're alike."

"No!" said Pettey, jumping to his feet. "I don't want just to be in Starfleet—I want to be the *best* that's ever been in Starfleet! I want to get through the Academy with top honors. I want to rise through the ranks faster than anyone. I want to command people like you."

Geordi was stunned for a moment by the cadet's fierce ambition. But he supposed ambition was just one more reason to join Starfleet. He hoped he would never be like Jack Pettey. "I wish you luck" was all he could think to say.

"I don't need luck," growled Pettey. "I need to be better than you. That's why I have to beat you tomorrow."

Geordi remarked, "I hope you're not too disappointed if you don't."

Pettey smiled. "We're not going to take it easy on you just because you're a bunch of . . ."

"Shrimps?" offered Kareem. "And we're not going to take it easy on you just because you're a bunch of jerks."

Pettey frowned. "We'll see you tomorrow. On the battlefield." With huge strides he bounded off into the darkness.

Jenna slammed her fist into her palm. "I really want to beat that guy."

"So do I," said Geordi. "But we have to remember that we've accomplished a lot. The worst we can finish is second, with two teams behind us."

"Geordi's right," said Kareem, and they all nodded their heads in agreement. "But it would be so much fun to beat them!" A cheer greeted that remark.

Geordi chuckled. "I don't know how much fun it's going to be tomorrow, but we've made our plans—now we have to execute them. Vernok, will you tell Zemusta to come in and get some rest? Keep your voices down, and brief him on our plans."

"Yes, sir," answered the little Saurian. He dashed off.

"You aren't worried about spies?" asked Jenna. "After that?"

"If they want to come over and watch us sleep, that's okay with me," said Geordi. "Because that's what we're going to do next. I want everybody to be well rested for tomorrow."

In silence they finished eating their dinner, then they retired to their tents. But saying they were going to sleep didn't make it so. Geordi lay awake, listening to Vernok purring softly beside him. *Maybe it would be good to be cold-blooded,* he thought.

"Geordi," said Kareem, "I can't sleep."

The captain sighed. "I know, but we've got to try. Whatever happens tomorrow, it's not going to help if we stay awake worrying about it."

"You're right," answered Kareem. "And no matter what happens tomorrow, I'm very proud to be on this team. This is what I dreamed of when I was accepted to the Academy."

"Winning?" asked Geordi.

"No. Competing as an equal."

Geordi smiled. "Get some sleep, my little brother. You'll need it."

After a few minutes he couldn't think of anything else to worry about. So Geordi took off his VISOR and surrendered to the complete darkness that engulfed him.

When Geordi emerged from his tent the next morning, he was troubled to see that the sky was gray and gloomy. He wanted it to be sunny like the day before—when they had won.

Altos seemed pleased with the gray sky. "Ah," said the Andorian, "a good day for battle."

Geordi looked at the coup meter on his chest, wondering if his luck would hold. Would he score a coup, or would he be captured today? If he was captured, would his team fight on or be demoralized?

He watched his teammates as they came out to eat their breakfast. Each of them looked determined and serious. No, thought Geordi, they would fight on no matter what happened to him personally. They knew this was the championship. They knew it was the last day of Capture the Flag. The last day of the Green team.

He remembered hearing that less than half of first-year cadets actually finished all four years of Starfleet Academy. He was saddened to think that some members of his team might not make it to Starfleet. Some of them would make it to Starfleet but discover they weren't cut out for such a demanding life. Some might even die while on duty in Starfleet.

Nobody could say what the future would bring for any of them. But today, right now, they had a chance to prove themselves.

They discussed the plans in hushed whispers, but nobody had any questions or doubts. They knew what they had to do. They were scared but relieved when Geordi's comm badge beeped.

"Pantano to La Forge," said the familiar voice. "Are you ready to beam up and start the game?"

Geordi looked around at his team and smiled. "We're ready."

CHAPTER

The importance of the championship was highlighted by the fact that Captain McKersie met them in the transporter room. The flight instructor was beaming as he greeted them.

"Congratulations to you, La Forge, and to the rest of your team," he said. "I'm looking forward to quite a match this morning."

"Thank you, sir," answered Geordi. He was glad somebody was enjoying the matches.

Lieutenant Pantano entered the room, carrying the Green and Gold flags. "Good morning," she said briskly. "Please step back while we bring the Gold team on board."

Geordi and his teammates did just that, and Geordi found that his heart was already beginning to beat uncomfortably fast.

"Energize," Pantano told the operator.

They watched as the Gold team materialized on the transporter platform. Geordi heard Megan gasp, and he could scarcely believe his VISOR. It appeared as if Jack Pettey and his team were wearing camouflage makeup on their faces.

"Are they wearing makeup?" he whispered to Jenna.

"Looks more like war paint," she answered. "They're just trying to scare us."

And they're doing a pretty good job of it, too, Geordi thought as he looked around at his team.

Pettey swaggered as he stepped off the transporter. "Captain McKersie, Lieutenant Pantano, it's an honor."

"My," said Pantano, "that is unusual paint you are wearing. How did you make it?"

"Charcoal, a little limestone, some clay," answered Pettey.

"Oh," said Kareem, "I thought you guys were just messy eaters."

The laughter that erupted from the Green team put them all back at ease. Geordi could've hugged the Neo-pygmy.

"We'll see who's laughing later," the big cadet warned them.

"Shake hands," said Emma Pantano. Her tone made it clear that was an order.

The teams shook hands, without much enthusiasm. Pettey saved a nasty glare and a firm handshake for Geordi.

Pantano handed the flag to Geordi and said, "The Green team was chosen at random to beam down first. Good luck to both of you."

"Thank you," answered Geordi. He had a feeling she was wishing his team a bit more luck.

Captain McKersie rubbed his hands together and grinned. "I'm looking forward to this. I'll see you in the lecture hall—the ones who are captured, of course." He strode out of the room.

Geordi looked at his teammates and nodded. They slowly took their places on the transporter platform.

"Coordinates locked in?" asked Pantano.

"Yes, sir."

"Energize."

They materialized in an unfamiliar part of the playing field. Perhaps, thought Geordi, it wasn't even the same playing field as the day before. Since what they had seen of Saffair all looked the same, there was no way of telling.

He handed the flag to Altos. "You know what to do."

"Yes, sir," said the big Andorian. His antennae twitched. "The flag is safe with me." He dashed off with tremendous leaps toward a boundary marker in the distance. Soon he was out of sight.

Geordi, T'Lara, and the others scanned the horizon, looking for a tall formation on which to plant the decoy.

"There," said Zemusta, pointing toward a weathered peak that could barely be seen against the gray sky. It wasn't as good as the archway they had defended the day before, thought Geordi, but it was the best they had.

"Let's all go over there," he said. "We want to see what direction they'll be coming from."

They began an earnest race toward the small peak, and Geordi, T'Lara, and Vernok scrambled to the top.

They found a small depression in which Vernok could sit. He turned his back on the playing field, craned his long neck downward, and held out his arm. His loose sleeve flapped in the breeze like a flag.

"Are you sure you can hold that position?" Geordi asked. It didn't look very comfortable.

The little Saurian managed a lopsided smile. "It was my idea, wasn't it? Please, just protect me. I don't want that blond ape jumping on my back."

Geordi nodded. "We'll do our best." He turned to survey the desolate plain. Thankfully, there was no sign yet of the Gold team. He hoped they, too, were having a hard time finding a place to put their flag.

"Captain," said T'Lara, "visibility is poorer today than yesterday. I believe their attackers will spot our decoy at about a hundred meters. That would put them on the far side of that small ravine. They should be running fairly fast as they try to cross it."

"So," said Geordi, "if we hide in the ravine, maybe we can catch them there. But where will they cross it?"

"That is a problem," the Vulcan agreed. "The farther away we mount the ambush, the more likely we will miss them. The closer to the decoy we mount it, the better our chance of success. However, you wished to have the battle in the middle of the field, away from the decoy."

Geordi was barely listening to her. He was beginning to worry about the time they were wasting. Here they were, doing the same thing that the losing Red and Blue teams had done—having a discussion when they should be taking action.

He pointed down to his teammates. "Kareem and

Zemusta," he ordered, "go out about half a kilometer and keep watch. I don't want them to surprise us."

"Yes, sir!" they answered.

They dashed off into the field, and Geordi felt better. But he still had a decision to make. If he made the wrong decision, it could be disastrous.

"All right," he said, "we'll plan the ambush in the ravine. If they run past us, we'll chase them down."

T'Lara nodded. Geordi almost wished she would make a comment—tell him whether he was right or wrong. But it wasn't in a Vulcan's character to question the decision of a superior. She leapt down to the ground.

Megan bounded up the rock and took her place near the little Saurian. She was already stripping leaves from a vine, and she used part of the vine to tie her hair back.

"I'll be very visible," she promised. "I'm making a wig out of these dark leaves."

Geordi gave her a feeble smile. He didn't know why, but his confidence was sagging. *Maybe we're being too tricky,* he thought. *Maybe we should just get out there and bump heads. We don't even know where our real flag is, we don't know where the enemy is, and we're planning an ambush!*

He pushed the doubts out of his mind and touched Megan's slim shoulder. "I'm sure you'll do fine. If this spot is overrun, get out of here, find Altos, and help him."

She nodded grimly. "Yes, sir."

Geordi jumped down from the rock and joined T'Lara and Jenna. He was beginning to worry about how they were so spread out: Altos with the real flag, Vernok and

Megan as the decoy, Zemusta and Kareem on watch, and only the three of them to mount the ambush.

"What's the matter?" asked Jenna.

He shook his head. "Just a lot on my mind."

"Don't worry," said Jenna. "We'll take them." She pointed to their companion. "See, T'Lara doesn't look worried."

The Vulcan remarked, "That is not within my capabilities."

Geordi had to chuckle. "All right, let's get down in that ravine."

With no more talk they raced about a hundred meters and hunkered down in a shallow ravine. Geordi looked at the ledge above them and hoped that the Gold team would leap over it without thinking. He looked back at the decoy and saw what looked like the Green flag and a dark-haired guard. The guard moved out of sight, and a few seconds later a white-haired guard appeared.

It looked convincing, thought Geordi, and he began to relax a little. T'Lara and Jenna took turns peering over the top of the ledge.

Suddenly, Geordi's communicator beeped. He held his breath and tapped it. "La Forge here."

A frightened breathless voice came. "It's Kareem! They snuck up on us! They're all over Zemusta, and they're chasing me!"

Geordi's throat tightened, but he calmly replied, "You know where to go. Lead them to it. Out."

Jenna looked stricken with worry. T'Lara peered over the ledge and remarked, "This may work to our advantage. Kareem could lead them directly into our ambush."

Geordi was up in a flash. "I see him!" he whispered. "We need to get about thirty meters to our left."

Running in a crouch, Geordi, Jenna, and T'Lara scuttled along the ravine. Geordi stole a glance over the ledge and saw a small Greenshirt with three Goldshirts fast behind him. Kareem was running for all he was worth, but his shorter legs doomed him against his bigger pursuers.

Jenna and T'Lara had passed Geordi and were moving into position. They looked back at him, and he motioned with his hands for them to stop. He peered over the top again and could see that the three Gold players were almost on top of Kareem.

Just a little bit farther, Kareem! Just a little bit more!

The brave Neo-pygmy dived over the ledge and sprawled in the ravine. At once a bald-headed Catullan was all over him, pounding his coup meter. Kareem vanished before anyone could do anything to help him. Just as quickly Jenna leapt out and grabbed the Gold player from behind in a bear hug. He disappeared in a swirling mass of light.

T'Lara was wrestling with another Goldshirt, a big Centaurian. Geordi feared she would lose the struggle, but her incredible strength allowed her to pin back his arms and brush his coup meter. He swung a fist at her chest, and she stumbled backward to get out of the way. His fist disappeared in midair, quickly followed by the rest of him.

The third Gold player, a bearded Argelian, threw Jenna to the ground and crawled on top of her, trying to reach her coup meter. Geordi rushed to help her, but

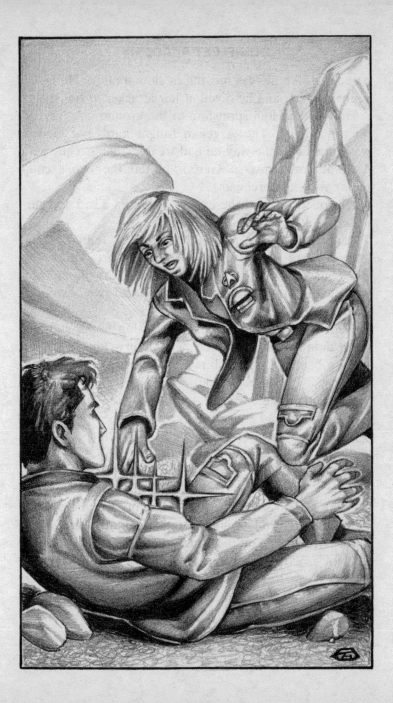

it seemed like he was moving in slow motion. He heard Jenna scream, and he dived at her attacker at full speed.

He knocked him sprawling to the ground and jumped on top of him. The Argelian fought hard, but Geordi was enraged at the way he had treated Jenna. They held each others' arms, so Geordi butted the man's coup meter with his forehead.

He rolled off, and the enemy gave him a sad and surprised look before he disappeared.

Panting, Geordi staggered to his feet. "Jenna ..." he gasped. "Are you all right?" He looked around.

"Jenna is gone," answered T'Lara. "But the ambush was successful. Counting Kareem, we lost two players to their three."

Geordi's heart sank. Somehow, losing Jenna and Kareem didn't seem like much of a victory. Plus, Zemusta was probably gone, which meant they were even—down to five players on each side.

His comm badge beeped, and he hoped for a moment that Zemusta had somehow escaped.

"La Forge here," he answered.

"Hi, Buddy. It's me, Jack Pettey."

"Huh?" asked Geordi. "How did you get on this channel?"

"Simple," answered Pettey. "I had my guys hold down that Tellarite, and I pulled off his comm badge. Then we zapped him. You're losing, buddy."

"Not exactly," answered Geordi. He was mad enough to lie. "You lost three guys yourself. That's three for you, and only one for me."

"What?" roared Pettey.

"Try to raise them. It was all planned—an ambush. You're outnumbered . . . buddy!"

Angrily Geordi banged his comm badge to turn it off. He didn't know what he was maddest about—losing his friends or Pettey's obnoxious attitude. Or maybe he was maddest about his own anger, and the way he had dispatched one of the Gold players.

T'Lara raised an eyebrow. "That was clever," she said. "We Vulcans do not lie, so we never realize what a tactical advantage lying can be."

"I'm not proud of it," muttered Geordi, brushing the green dirt off his pants. "Now what?"

T'Lara peered across the deserted plain. "If they think we have an advantage, will they be more cautious? Or more reckless? You know human behavior better than I."

Geordi shrugged. "It's hard for me to think like Pettey. But my guess is that he's very angry. He'll want to find *me.*"

"If that is the case," said T'Lara, "then you should station yourself with Megan at the decoy. The combination of seeing you and our flag may prove irresistible to Cadet Pettey. He may expend what is left of his resources attacking it."

"And what will you be doing?" asked Geordi.

"Somebody must locate their flag and see how many are guarding it."

Geordi sighed. "Yeah, you're right. All of that makes a lot of sense. Despite what Pettey thinks, we've only got five people, and we've got to use them wisely. But take the long way around, and don't let them spot you."

T'Lara nodded. "My intention is not to be captured."

The Vulcan got down in a crouch and ran back along the ravine until she was out of sight, her green tunic and green-tinged skin helping her to blend in. If she was out of his sight, thought Geordi, he could only hope that she was out of Pettey's sight, too.

He still felt worried and glum as he made his way back to the decoy. He missed Jenna and Kareem. Of course, both of them had been captured in yesterday's game, and they had still won. But he had watched that from a distance. Today it had happened right in front of him—with him unable to stop it.

It was true, they weren't really gone. They were sitting in comfortable seats right now, sipping lemonade and watching him on the viewscreen. But he felt like a captain who had lost valuable members of his crew.

Maybe that's the true purpose of this game, thought Geordi. *It's not the strategy or the combat—but to make us realize what it feels like to lose our comrades. Our friends.*

Geordi knew from the years he had spent growing up on starships that mistakes often caused death. Real death, where people didn't come back. Now all of the cadets would know it. Even Jack Pettey must have felt the loss of those three teammates he had sent into an ambush. After this, would he be so anxious to command?

Megan waved to him as he climbed slowly up the limestone formation. He was impressed by the way Vernok was still holding his position, still looking like a flag.

"Is everything okay?" asked Megan.

Geordi shrugged. "I think so. Jenna, Kareem, and Zemusta are gone, but so are three of their people. Our advantage is that they think we have seven players, and we know they only have five."

"Why did you come back?" asked Vernok without moving a muscle.

"Jack Pettey is angry at me. If he sees me up here, he might try to rush us with everything he's got. T'Lara is still out there, looking for their flag."

"Well," said Megan, "I think your plan is working."

"What?" asked Geordi.

Megan pointed off into the distance. Three Goldshirts were headed toward them, moving fast.

CHAPTER

Geordi backed up and nearly fell over Vernok. "Sorry," he said. He looked at Megan. "Have you made any nets?"

"Only one," she answered. "I was doing it mostly for show."

"Okay," said Geordi. "Find a good hiding place, and be ready to use it. There's three of us and three of them."

"But one of us is a flag," Vernok reminded him.

"At the right moment," said Geordi, "you can stop being a flag."

He leaned over and watched Megan scamper down the rock formation and squeeze herself into a crevice. Then he looked across the plain. The three Gold players were closing rapidly, led by a big cadet with golden hair.

Geordi suddenly felt very alone atop the rock. He wished he could trade places with Altos, wherever he was.

There was no doubt Pettey would attack them. He would conclude that he had three attackers to their two defenders. He would assume the rest of the Green team was after his flag, which would make an attack even more urgent.

Geordi quickly planned his strategy. He knew he had to make sure they attacked from the front, where Megan was hidden. From the front, they could only see Vernok's back. If they attacked from the side or the rear, they might find out they were being tricked.

Finally the three Goldshirts slowed to a jog and stopped at the bottom of the rock. Sweat had darkened their camouflage paint, and they looked as if they had been rolling in the dirt.

"Not too close," the Gold captain warned his teammates. "They might have nets."

"Yeah, that's right!" Geordi yelled down. "Stay away from us—unless you want to go back and watch this on a viewscreen!"

Pettey smiled. "You may have more players than we do, although I'm beginning to doubt it. But we found your flag first! My defenders haven't seen any of your people!"

"They won't see them, until it's too late!"

That made Pettey pause in thought. He motioned his players to come close and hear his whispered orders. They nodded and started to circle the rock.

"Are you afraid?" taunted Geordi. "Where are you going?"

"Just going to take a look around," said Pettey.

"This is it!" shouted Geordi. "Are you saying the three of you can't climb up here and take this flag away from me?"

"We know there's at least one more of you!" snapped Pettey.

"Oh!" scoffed Geordi. "Then you're scared of *two* of us?"

Pettey scowled. Geordi knew he was beginning to strike home. He played his dirtiest card. "If you're too much of a coward, Jack, send the other two! Like you did yesterday!"

That got all three humans climbing up the front face of the rock. Pettey started out in the lead, but he was smarter than the other two. He slowed down and let them pass him while he watched their progress.

The first one who got to Megan's hiding place didn't even see her until it was too late. She whipped the net around his arms, and he was about to fall when she slapped his coup meter. By the time he lost his balance, he was disappearing.

His comrade moved swiftly and grabbed her arm. Megan struggled, but she was slight and not very strong. It was all she could do to keep from falling. Somehow, she kept her feet in the crevice and battled the attacker.

Geordi wanted to help her, but he knew he dared not move. He had to pretend that the flag was behind him, and he couldn't desert it—not even to save the albino cadet. He watched with dismay as Pettey came to help capture her.

Megan finally did the only thing she could—she leapt from the rock and tumbled to the ground. The Goldshirt

was right behind her, and he landed on her back. She squirmed out from under him, and they both turned to attack. They hit each others' coup meters at the same time.

And they vanished in twin columns of dancing light.

Jack Pettey laughed, as if he was expecting this. "Okay, La Forge, it's just you and me! The two captains!"

"It would appear so," agreed Geordi.

Pettey was still wary as he climbed up the rock. He was half expecting someone else to jump out of a crevice with a net. But that wasn't the surprise that was waiting for him, Geordi knew. The smaller cadet edged closer to the edge, hoping he could hit Pettey's coup meter when he tried to climb over.

But the Gold captain was ready for that maneuver. He grinned at Geordi for a moment, then threw a handful of dirt and pebbles into his face. Geordi flung his arms in front of his face to protect his VISOR, and he stumbled backward. By the time he scrambled to his feet, Pettey was standing in front of him, laughing.

Geordi instantly positioned himself between Pettey and the fake flag. He marveled at the way Vernok was still holding perfectly still. Pettey had to keep his eyes on Geordi and couldn't take a good look at the flag.

He came closer, and Geordi took a swing at his coup meter. The bigger cadet jumped back.

"You're done now," said Pettey.

"We'll see," rasped Geordi.

In a flash Pettey bounded on top of him and grabbed his arms. Geordi fought for all he was worth, but the cadet was much bigger and stronger. He held Geordi's arms in a viselike grip. As he had done to the other Gold player, Geordi tried to butt Pettey's coup meter with his head. The big cadet shook him like a rag.

In a judo move, Pettey swung a foot behind Geordi's leg and dropped him to the ground. Geordi was stunned and couldn't move. He saw Pettey's hand sweeping down toward his chest and barely managed to deflect it. It missed his coup meter by a centimeter.

Pettey cursed and tried again, but Geordi quickly rolled over. The blow hit him hard in the back. He stumbled forward, but the cadet jumped on his legs and pinned him to the ground.

He's not going after the flag, thought Geordi, *until he*

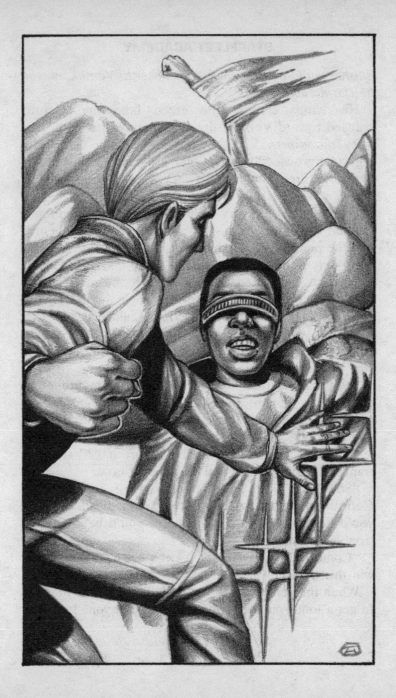

finishes with me. If I can just get closer to Vernok, maybe he can do something!

His hands clawing the green limestone, Geordi crawled toward Vernok, dragging Pettey after him. *Just a few more meters!* As they got closer to the decoy, the big cadet growled like an animal, gripped Geordi's shoulders, and threw him onto his back. Geordi struggled, but Pettey was too strong and too determined.

With a howl of victory he hit Geordi's coup meter and jumped to his feet. In his last second on Saffair, Geordi had the pleasure of watching Pettey reach for the Green flag—only to have it leap up and strike him in the chest.

"Aargh!" screamed the big cadet as he materialized next to Geordi in the transporter room of the *Glenn*. "No! No! That flag was alive! How could it be?"

Geordi was still panting as he stepped off the transporter. But he was also grinning. "That wasn't a flag—it was Vernok!"

"Not the Saurian!" yelled Pettey. His mouth hung open. "You planted a decoy! Where's your real flag?"

Geordi shook his head. "To tell you the truth, I don't know."

"Can't you guys argue in the lecture hall?" said the transporter operator. "You're out of it now."

"Sorry, sir," said Pettey to the ensign. He glared at Geordi for a moment, then just shook his head. "I knew you'd be trouble, but I didn't know you'd be *this much* trouble."

"Come on!" said Geordi. "Let's see who's going to win this thing."

When they entered the lecture hall, they were amazed to get a loud round of applause from everyone gathered

106

there. Captain McKersie was beaming, and Lieutenant Pantano nodded her head in approval. Jenna, Kareem, and the other Green players were laughing.

"Excellent play!" barked Captain McKersie.

Sidra Swan rushed up to Geordi and shook his hand. "I don't know if you're going to win or not, but we're all rooting for you."

"Thanks," he muttered. He looked around the room and saw, to his amazement, that most of the audience did seem to be rooting for the Green team. And he thought nobody liked his bunch of oddballs.

Geordi was also surprised to find out that he could be captured and still be a hero. He looked over at Jack Pettey, thinking how ironic it was that they were both out of action. Only their plans and a few teammates survived. The measure of good officers, Geordi knew, was not how they performed, but how their crew performed when they weren't around.

"What's going on?" growled Jack Pettey, taking a seat in the front row.

One of his teammates reported, "They've got three players to our two. Our two are where you stationed them, guarding the flag. The Vulcan has it under observation, and the Saurian is coming to help her. The Andorian is guarding their *real* flag."

"Not for long," said Kareem. "Look!"

He pointed to the left screen, where the Andorian was sitting calmly in front of the Green flag. He spoke into his communicator and stood up.

"They've told him to come for the final battle," said Jenna. "There's nobody to go after the Green flag now."

Jack Pettey began to chew on a fingernail. "I don't like this," he muttered. "I don't like this at all."

By contrast Geordi was rather enjoying being a spectator. He had enough cuts and bruises to show that he had played—and played hard. He slumped into a seat and was soon surrounded by his captured teammates, Jenna, Megan, Kareem, and Zemusta. Jenna brought him a glass of lemonade.

She grinned. "The decoy worked like a charm."

"But it's not over yet," remarked Zemusta. The Tellarite crinkled his snout with worry.

There were a few minutes of calm as the Andorian bounded across the plain to join his comrades, T'Lara and Vernok. Glancing from one screen to another, Geordi had to smile. One of the Gold defenders was a Delosian and the other was a Betazoid, which meant there were no humans left in the game.

He looked again at Jack Pettey, and the big cadet shrugged and shook his head. Yes, he noticed it, too—the fate of the game was up to a bunch of nonhumans.

All eyes and one VISOR were soon drawn to the right-hand screen. Everyone knew what had to come next—an assault on the Gold flag. As before, the Gold team had planted it on level ground right in front of a boundary marker. There was only one way to approach it.

They couldn't hear T'Lara's orders, because she whispered them. A moment later she and Altos stood and walked confidently toward the two Gold defenders. Vernok trailed behind them. The defenders stood shoulder to shoulder directly in front of their flag. They got down in wrestling crouches, ready to meet the attack.

There were no taunts or shouts this time. No trickery. Looking very determined, Altos and T'Lara broke into a run and leapt upon the defenders.

The Gold players fought valiantly and wrestled the attackers away from their flag. But there was no one to stop the little Saurian. Vernok slipped between the grunting warriors and grabbed the prize! With a strange chirp he waved the Gold flag over his head.

A buzzer sounded in the lecture hall, followed by deafening cheers. Everyone crowded around Geordi, slapping his shoulders and pumping his hands.

"Good job!"

"Wonderful strategy!"

"Three cheers for our captain!"

Captain McKersie shook his hand. "Keep this up, Mr. La Forge, and you have quite a future ahead of you."

"Thank you, sir."

Geordi looked past his well-wishers at Jack Pettey, who sat alone, dejected. The big cadet buried his face in his hands. Geordi now knew why he never liked gym class and competitive sports. He liked to win, but he hated to see other people lose.

"Thank you, thank you," he said to everyone as he gently shoved past them. He finally ended up in front of Jack Pettey. The others in the room seemed to melt away.

The blond young man muttered, "If you've come to gloat, go ahead. I deserve it."

"Yes, you do," Geordi agreed. "But I'm not much good at gloating. I'd rather make friends." He smiled and held out his hand.

Pettey looked at him with surprise. Then a grin crept across his face, and he pumped Geordi's hand. "If I ever get to command—I know that's a big *if*—I'm going to remember this day. I'm going to remember that brute force doesn't always work. You've got to use your brain—and your heart."

The big cadet stood up. "You're a classy guy, La Forge. I want you on my team next time."

Geordi smiled. "Then choose me first."

Pettey grinned. "I will—after I choose that little Saurian."

Capture the Flag

The Red team won the afternoon match for third place, which pleased Geordi. He felt happy for Sidra Swan. But he couldn't really pay much attention to the game, because everyone was so busy congratulating him. It felt strange to be a hero.

After leaving orbit, the first-year cadets got a detailed tour of the *Glenn,* which was almost as exciting as the game. Later that night Captain McKersie repeated the video log of the championship match for the upperclass cadets, who hadn't been able to watch it live. But Geordi left shortly after the beginning. He didn't want to see his friends be captured, and he didn't want to see his new friends lose.

A party was going on in the lounge, but Geordi didn't stay long. He went to his room, read a journal, and dropped off to sleep as soon as his head hit the pillow.

CHAPTER
11

Two days later Geordi stood on the bank of the stream that meandered through the grounds at Starfleet Academy. It was the same stream, the same buildings, the same classrooms, and the same teachers. But everything else was different.

Was it him? He didn't feel any different. But there was something in the way people talked to him, the way they treated him, even the way they looked at him. People he didn't know, like that fellow named William Riker, came up and introduced themselves. It was all different.

He thought about the way his life had been only a week earlier. He hardly had any friends then—he didn't even know anybody's name! Now everybody said hello to him. He was going to a concert tonight with Megan, and tomorrow he was going to a football game with Jenna. Women were still something of a mystery, but at least they were a friendly mystery.

Now if he could just find time to study!

"La Forge!" called a cranky voice.

Geordi jumped and checked his feet. "I'm not walking on the liverwort!" he answered.

"I know you're not," said Boothby. The old gardener strode up to him and smiled. "In fact, I hear you walk on water now."

"That's not true," said Geordi, shaking his head. "Does everybody on campus know about it?"

"That you won Capture the Flag?" asked Boothby. "Of course they know. I heard you took a bunch of losers and molded them into a fighting force to be reckoned with."

"Bah," scoffed Geordi. "I just got lucky. I chose those people just to prove a point. They're the ones who did it, not me."

Boothby shrugged. "Nevertheless, they'll be watching you now. They'll expect more from you. They'll want to get you on the fast track to a command post."

Geordi moaned. "I don't want to command—I want to be an engineer, or a navigator."

"Maybe you'll command an engineering department," said Boothby. "Next to the Bridge, that's the most important part of a starship."

Geordi nodded thoughtfully. "Yeah, maybe."

The old man squinted, as if he was remembering something. "Years ago, there was another cadet who was having trouble at the Academy until he won a parrises squares tournament. His name was Picard."

"Who?"

"Never mind. You haven't heard about him yet, but you will. Listen, La Forge, don't let them push you into anything. You're still the master of your own fate."

The young cadet shrugged. "I never felt that way before—like I was the master of my own fate."

"Well, you proved that you are," said Boothby. "You made them notice you, and that's a rare achievement here. Unless it's for something bad."

Geordi chuckled. "I'm not complaining. It was a good experience for all of us."

"Just remember one thing," growled Boothby.

"Yes?"

"Stay off my liverwort."

About the Author

JOHN VORNHOLT was born in Marion, Ohio, and knew he wanted to write science fiction when he discovered Doc Savage novels and the works of Edgar Rice Burroughs. But somehow he wrote nonfiction and television scripts for many years, including animated series such as *Dennis the Menace, Ghostbusters,* and *Super Mario Brothers.* He was also an actor and playwright, with several published plays to his credit.

John didn't get back to his first love—writing SF—until 1989 with the publication of his first Star Trek Next Generation novel, *Masks.* He wrote two more, *Contamination* and *War Drums;* a classic Trek novel, *Sanctuary;* and a Deep Space Nine novel, *Antimatter.* For young readers, he's also written nonfiction books and the novel *How to Sneak into the Girls' Locker Room.*

John lives in Tucson, Arizona, with his wife, Nancy, his children, Sarah and Eric, and his dog, Bessie.

About the Illustrator

TODD CAMERON HAMILTON is a self-taught artist who has resided all his life in Chicago, Illinois. He has been a professional illustrator for the past ten years, specializing in fantasy, science fiction, and horror. His original works grace many private and corporate collections. He has co-authored two novels and several short stories. When not drawing, painting, or writing, his interests include metalsmithing, puppetry, and teaching.

BLAST OFF ON NEW ADVENTURES FOR THE YOUNGER READER!

A new title every other month!

Pocket Books presents two new young adult series based on the hit television shows, STAR TREK: THE NEXT GENERATION® and STAR TREK®: DEEP SPACE NINE™

Before they became officers aboard the <u>U.S.S. Enterprise</u>™, your favorite characters struggled through the Academy....

STARFLEET ACADEMY™

#1: WORF'S FIRST ADVENTURE
#2: LINE OF FIRE
#3: SURVIVAL
by Peter David

#4: CAPTURE THE FLAG
by John Vornholt

#5: ATLANTIS STATION
by V.E. Mitchell
(Coming in mid-July 1994)

TM, ® & © 1994 Paramount Pictures. All Rights Reserved.

Published by Pocket Books

928-04